ꟷꟷꟷꟷ

The alarm clock buzzed. Cheerio, one eye squeezed shut and the other a slit, reached over and slapped at it groggily. "Good Monday morning, Cheerio Monroe!" Mindy said brightly. The greeting was followed by a kiss and squeeze on a sleek thigh and a quickie attack session.

"Are you finished with me yet?" Cheerio panted afterwards.

"You may go," Mindy said, waving a hand in dismissal. Cheerio staggered into the bathroom to shower and get ready for work.

During breakfast, Cheerio said, "What's with you? You have me when we go to bed, you wake me up around three to have me, and you have me again first thing in the morning."

Mindy poked a foot under the table and between Cheerio's knees and mournfully said, "I know. The honeymoon must be over if we're only making love three times a day."

You Light
the Fire

You Light the Fire

Kristen Garrett

RISING
TIDE
PRESS

5 KIVY ST.,
HUNTINGTON STATION,
N.Y. 11746

Rising Tide Press
5 Kivy Street
Huntington Station, NY 11746

The publishers wished to thank all of the friends who helped to make this book possible: Edna G., Adriane B., Pat G., Harriet E., Marie H., Beth H., Bobbi B., and Evelyn R. We love you.

Printed in the United States

Publisher's note:
All characters, places and situations in this book are fictitious and any resemblance to persons (living or dead) is purely coincidental.

First printing July, 1992
10 9 8 7 6 5 4 3 2

Edited by Alice Frier and Lee Boojamra
Book cover design and illustration by Evelyn Rysdyk

Library of Congress Cataloging-in-Publication Data

Garrett, Kristen, 1955-
        You Light the Fire/ by Kristen Garrett
            p.cm

ISBN 0-9628938-5-4

                                        92-060176
                                        CIP

Acknowledgements

Thanks to Amanda for being positive when times were tough. H.B., your contribution and support can't be measured. Thanks to various people throughout the country for putting up with the long-distance neurotic fits at three in the morning. And to my editor, Lee Boojamra, in addition to the heartfelt appreciation and gratitude, I offer the following good-natured jeer: what time is it?

Biographical Sketch

Kristen Garrett attended college on a partial academic scholarship, supplemented by working nights as a waitress, and eventually earned a Masters degree. Since graduation she has worked as an educator for fifteen years. She likes guinea pigs and wild squirrels and pizza and driving fast. Kristen and life-mate presently live in the mountains of the Southeastern United States.

For Lin. You took away my hungry heart and gave meaning to everything I do.

CHAPTER 1

"I'd like to make this a collect call," the brown-eyed beauty said, standing in a phone booth and sweltering in the August heat. "My name is Melinda Sue Brinson. Mindy. Tell them it's Mindy." She ran her fingers through her auburn hair as she waited for the call to go through. Her hair, long and glossy, felt greasy. But anyone would feel like a grease-ball after twelve hours on the road, wedged into a silver 1971 Ford Mustang fastback with all her possessions. Greasy though she might be, she was too excited to be tired. Tulsa was absolutely huge. The metropolitan area population was over half a million people. She was shocked at the difference between her new home and her old one, Hopkinsville, Kentucky, population twenty-seven thousand three hundred eighteen.

"Yes, I'll accept the call," Mother said, sounding depressed.

"You should see Tulsa!" Mindy exclaimed. "There's so many lights. And cars. The traffic is horrible. All the streets are four-lane, except for the ones that are six-lane or eight-lane. It's absolutely unbelievable. Everywhere you look are cars and lights and stores. And people, lawsy mercy, you should see the people!"

"I can't believe you actually up and went out there," Mother choked. "I felt like a bomb had bursted on my head this morning when you left. Are you ready to come home yet?"

Mindy could tell Mother was crying. Probably been blubbering all day. "I've explained to you at least fifteen times why I *had* to move here," Mindy said impatiently. "I can make more money, there's more room for advancement, and a bigger school system will be more of a challenge. Hello? Hello? Mother? Are you there?"

Daddy's voice came over the phone. "Your mother can't talk," he said. "She's crying. You know, she said she wasn't even going to change the sheets on your bed. She said they still smell like your perfume."

"That's silly. Mother doesn't even like my perfume."

"So what will you do now?"

Mindy knew Daddy was wondering if his little girl was frightened half to death. They were probably packed and ready to catch a plane to Oklahoma to bring their baby home. "I've got everything planned," she said confidently. "First, I'm going to check into a motel. In the morning I'll interview for my job. I'll find an apartment in the afternoon. I passed a complex driving into Tulsa that had a sign advertising fireplaces and ceiling fans and low rent. There's a housing surplus here."

"What if you don't get the job?"

"I'll get the job," Mindy said. She couldn't stand negative thinking. "It's mine. I can feel it. Besides, I doubt they'd ask a young hotshot like me to drive all this way just to tell me no."

The phone was quiet for a long time. "I suppose you will get hired," Daddy finally said. "You usually get what you want. Do you miss us?"

"Of course," Mindy said. "What kind of question is that?"

"We love you."

"Me, too, Daddy. I'll call tomorrow to let you know what high school I'll be teaching at."

*****

Mindy frowned when the man inside the Best Western told her a room was sixty dollars for one night. Not wanting to seem a small-town clod, she paid without complaining. Her car was parked right outside the door so she could keep an eye on it. She hadn't brought much with her, but she sure didn't want what she did have to get stolen. Not after she'd already been ripped-off by the motel itself. Sixty dollars for a shower and a night's sleep! She couldn't believe it!

She laughed when she saw her face in the mirror above the dresser in her room. Basketball-sized brown eyes. Eleven freckles across the bridge of her nose. Her mouth was practically a foot wide. She looked as tired and greasy as she felt.

Mindy wasn't stupid. She knew her face looked like the one next-door that every boy gets a crush on at one time or another. Beginning her sophomore year in high school, she'd grown used to hearing boys whisper, "Look at the ass on that one, will you? Is she built like a brick outhouse, or what?" as she walked past on her way to class.

Invariably, another boy would say, "Hey, go talk to her. I hear she don't mind puttin' out if ya catch her in the right mood."

Another boy would say, "Are you kiddin'? I ain't talkin' to her. She's a squirrel. I never know what she's talkin' 'bout. I don't care if she puts out or not. It ain't worth it."

Mindy always ignored the whispers because she knew what the boys were talking about, even if they never knew what she was talking about. She'd never cared that much for boys who used both gross and improper English and were six inches shorter than her, anyway.

It was about the same time she had her first sexual experience. Although, actually, she'd been more like a spectator with the best seat in the house, instead of one of the players. The great event happened in the back seat of a black Chevrolet Caprice. She was barely fifteen years old. The boy's name was Billy Marchant.

On the night in question, she was lying in Billy's back seat admiring the full moon, halfheartedly listening to his enthused panting and slapping at his wandering hands with more enthusiasm. She was resigned when he unzipped her jeans and slipped a hand inside her panties.

Then Billy started tugging at her jeans.

3

Mindy held onto her jeans and frowned. "Just what do you think you're doing?" she asked, as if it wasn't completely obvious what Billy thought he was doing.

Billy grinned. He was a senior and the captain of the basketball team, so he was highly coveted by all the girls, although Mindy couldn't understand why. He seemed more than a little oily to her and he usually smelled like jock-itch powder. "If you don't, I'm going to tell everyone you did, even if you didn't," Billy said. "If you do, then I'll tell everyone you didn't, even if you did."

"You're not making sense."

"This is how these things work," Billy explained matter-of-factly. "Not only will I tell everyone at school you did if you don't, I'm also going to tell your parents you did. But if you do, then I'll tell your parents you didn't if they should ever ask if you have or not."

"It somehow seems strange to me that I *will* get in trouble for *not* doing something Mother has implied is wrong," Mindy said. "It also seems strange that I *won't* get in trouble for *doing* something Mother has implied is wrong." She looked at Billy. "I really wish you'd just go away. Take your double negatives with you. They give me a headache. No wonder you flunked English last semester."

Billy grinned again, doing a fairly good impersonation of a mad opossum. Mindy said, "On top of everything else, I just happen to know a girl can go to a doctor and have an examination to find out for sure if she has or hasn't. I think maybe you don't know what you're talking about..., but you sure know what you're doing."

Billy snickered and kissed her neck.

Mindy twisted a strand of hair around a finger and looked out the rear window at the full moon. She started thinking of all the other girls all across America. Really, all the other girls in the world. She wondered how many girls were in the same situation at the same time she was? How many girls in the back seats of sleds in Russia? How many girls in the back seats of gondolas in Italy? How many girls in the back seats of rickshas in China? Did these other girls love the boy who was forcing himself on them? Or was he only someone like Billy Marchant was to her? Someone she dated partly so she could be just like all her friends who always had a date on Saturday night, and mostly because her parents insisted she date boys.

It was funny, really. All these girls, all under the same full moon, all tightly clutching their jeans and squeezing their thighs together against the intrusion of an insistent, wheedling boy, all in the same situation at the same time. As she looked at the full moon and thought about the other girls, she started wondering how many miles past the moon outer space extended. Then she started thinking about how high an exponent it would take to put the miles into a workable number. Next she started wondering how big an exponent she could calculate in her head. She started at eight to the third.

The next thing she knew, her jeans were absent without leave, Billy's bare, flexing bottom was between her legs, her left breast was in his mouth, and the situation had climaxed while she was somewhere between eight to the fourth and eight to the fifth. She was surprised when it didn't hurt. She always thought it would hurt. But it didn't. Not anymore than going to the dentist, anyway.

She had a screaming fight with Billy on the way home from The Great Double Negative Debate because she didn't like what he'd done to her, not one little bit, and they parted mortal enemies. The next week, as if by magic, whispers began to circulate around Hopkinsville High. Whispers about how she let you-know-who suck this and stroke that and how she was frigid because she hadn't done anything except lie there on her back with a blank expression on her face and a crotch as dry as a tobacco field during a drought.

Mindy knew where the whispers had started, but she didn't confront anyone, other than to say maybe she'd just lain there with a blank expression on her face and a crotch as dry as a tobacco field during a drought because she didn't know what else to do once she saw a mosquito stinger where a boy's pecker should've been. In the end, she decided everyone could kiss her bottom and she ignored the whispers because, fact was, they were mostly the truth. Still, she was confused because she *had*, and Billy told everyone, even after he promised he wouldn't if she did.

Confused, yes, but she wasn't a fool. She learned from the experience. She learned to never, ever, try calculating exponents in her head if someone's hand was in her panties. At such times it really didn't matter how far past the moon outer space extended. Not to the other person, anyway.

Shortly after The Great Double Negative Debate, she was loafing around in the basement game room of her Baptist church, halfheartedly rolling the nine ball from one end of the pool table to the other and feeling practically forlorn over being the latest locker room topic. All of a sudden she heard a sound, looked up and saw the nineteen year old pixieish brunette daughter of the church's cleaning lady. Her name was Corrine.

Corrine closed and locked the door. She walked to the pool table and said, "You good-looking heifer, I've seen the way you go around all moon-eyed, cutting your eyes at every girl that comes within ten miles. Why you wasting time on boys?"

Mindy mumbled something about how she didn't want to go out with boys, but her parents made her. Corrine said, "The hell with your parents. There's ways to make boys leave you alone. Putting out pussy like I hear you did the other night isn't one."

Mindy blushed clear down to her toenails.

Corrine unbuttoned her blouse, unzipped her jeans and said, "I've seen the way you gawk at me. You like me, don't you?"

Mindy's eyes popped practically clear out of her face when she saw Corrine's breasts inside her unbuttoned blouse because Corrine wasn't wearing a bra. And then she saw the dark hair curling inside Corrine's unzipped Levi's because Corrine wasn't wearing panties.

Mindy's legs carried her and the nine ball she was clutching closer. "If I could just look at you," she offered. "Maybe touch you."

Corrine smirked. She traced a fingernail along the back of Mindy's hand. "You're lying," Corrine said. "I see what's in your eyes. You want more than looking and touching." She took the nine ball from Mindy's hands and tossed it onto the pool table with a thud.

A few grunting, frantic seconds later, Mindy was naked on the pool table with Corrine and the nine ball, tasting the spot where a girl is wettest, having her own sopping wet spot tasted, and crowing like a rooster at sunrise. Her first ever orgasm practically blew off the top of her head.

Afterwards, while they were rebuttoning and rezipping and brushing hair, Corrine said, "You just learned the difference between making love and giving a boy a piece of ass. Quit wasting time on them. You're a dyke. A lesbian. Like me. Have you heard them words before?"

"No," Mindy said. "When can we make love again? I'm ready right now."

"Not with me," Corrine replied, giving Mindy a kiss. "You're jailbait, honey. I taught you the basics. Find someone your own age to learn the rest with." A few days later, Corrine ran off with the wife of the assistant deputy mayor.

Mindy was practically heartbroken to hear about Corrine's running away so soon after their pool-table-tryst, but, still, since she wasn't a fool, she learned from the experience. She learned tasting wetness and crowing like a rooster was a lot more fun than twisting hair and calculating exponents. She also looked dyke/lesbian up in the dictionary and realized that's exactly who she was, so she quit wasting time on boys and went to looking for someone her own age to learn about making love with, like Corrine had told her.

CHAPTER 2

After six weeks in Tulsa, Mindy felt so metropolitan and adult and self-sufficient that it was practically disgusting. Especially when she sat in her apartment and knew the rent for the month was paid. Her apartment was small and sparsely furnished, but it was cozy with the warm beige carpet and miniature fireplace and the three house plants she'd bought at Target. It was convenient, as well, since it was only three miles from the high school. School was going good, too; she liked all her classes and most of her students. On top of everything else, her car had a new tune-up and two new tires, and she had $53.18 in cold, hard cash in her purse.

Life would be perfect if only she didn't have to beat all her lovers off with a stick.

Mindy giggled at herself. Truth was she hadn't crawled between the sheets with anyone in Tulsa. She hadn't even met anyone other than the other teachers at school, and none of them were people she really wanted to be after-work-friends with because most of them were lots older than her and had different interests. And none of the other teachers were lesbians, not that she could tell, anyway. She saw lots of good-looking women everywhere she went in Tulsa, though, and she knew some of them *had* to be lesbians. But they never spoke to her and she was too bashful to start talking first. She didn't start a conversation with the good-looking women she saw because she just knew they would say, "Take a gander at those huge bean-fed thunder thighs and that broad grits-fed bottom," the second they laid eyes on her.

Lawsy, was she lying to herself or what! She didn't feel bashful around city women because she thought she was fat. She could walk through a rainstorm and not get wet, if it wasn't for her 36D's. She only weighed one hundred and forty-five pounds, which wasn't all that much for someone who was seventy-three inches tall. Truth was, she was bashful around city women because she was afraid they would laugh at her once they recognized what a healthy but provincial and unsophisticated small-town clod she was.

Another truth was, though she'd never admit it to anyone, she sometimes noticed her hand, wrapped in a soapy washcloth, lingering longer than necessary between her legs when she showered. She tried to make her hand stop. But she couldn't, her hand knew what she liked. She'd end up stretched out in the bathtub, gritting her teeth and kicking her feet as the hot water squirted in her face. She was *so* embarrassed for her body. What a selfish thing to do. Giving herself to herself. She tried to rationalize by saying she was a human being, after all, and her body had needs even if her mind tried to ignore them. But she was still embarrassed.

*****

Mindy grabbed her shopping list and drove to Skaggs, the grocery store closest to her apartment. Five minutes later she made a total bottom-hole of herself, an occurrence that surprised her not in the slightest since she'd known it was only a matter of time until she made a total bottom-hole of herself at Skaggs. The only thing that surprised her was it took so long.

Lust was the reason she made a complete fool of herself at Skaggs. She was pushing her cart around a corner, when she bumped carts with a living doll. The living doll had brown hair and an exquisite set of delicate ankles and smelled absolutely heavenly. "Hi, there," Mindy leered, feeling like the wolf talking to Little Red Riding Hood.

The living doll clutched Mindy's hand and giggled and said, "I'm a terrible driver. I'm running into people constantly." Her hand was moist and soft. Her fingernails were polished a darling shade of pink.

Mindy giggled, too, and admitted she wasn't all that good a driver, either. They started chatting about the weather and high grocery prices and such. While they chatted, they cast snoopy sidelong glances into each other's carts to see what the other was buying.

After a few minutes of chatting and snooping, Mindy touched the living doll's hand and practically purred, "I don't know anybody in Tulsa. I haven't lived here very long. Do you think we could get together later? For a movie? Or a drink? Maybe we could go dancing. I like dancing."

The living doll practically dropped her teeth. "That's sickening!" she snapped. "I don't know why they let people like you out in public! I'm telling the manager!"

"I-I-I'm sorry," Mindy stammered, wishing she could sink through the floor. "You acted so friendly, I..."

The living doll whipped her cart around and sped off at the speed of outrage, roaring for the manager every step of the way. Mindy snatched up her shopping list and got the dickens out of Skaggs, leaving her groceries sitting in the cart at the end of the noodle-bean-spaghetti sauce aisle. Her face felt absolutely on fire. She couldn't believe she'd made a blatant pass at a straight woman. She was more or less confused about how the living doll had acted, too. Mindy hadn't committed murder. She'd only made a blatant pass. All the living doll had to do was say no and walk away instead of running around roaring for the store manager.

She drove across the street to Safeway and bought her groceries there, although she normally didn't like Safeway because she thought their prices were higher than Skaggs'. Her lusting eyes she kept to herself and her blatant mouth she kept shut the whole time she was in Safeway.

You Light The Fire

When she came out of the store, with the sack boy rattling along behind with her groceries, she saw the living doll again, standing beside a black BMW parked four spaces from Mindy's car. Mindy practically chortled. Head-games. She liked mental foreplay. The living doll waited until Mindy's groceries were tucked away in her trunk before approaching. "I'm sorry," the living doll said when she was maybe three feet away.

"My name's Melinda Sue Brinson." Mindy offered her hand.

"I'm Kim."

"Want to come over while I put my things away?" Mindy suggested. "I live not far from here. We can have a nice chat." She felt excited about entertaining her first friend in her apartment.

"I'll follow you," Kim murmured demurely since she liked playing games.

*****

Mindy put her things away, fixed two cups of herb tea and joined Kim on the couch, sitting maybe two millimeters away. Close enough that their thighs touched. Kim said, "I'm sorry about what happened at Skaggs."

"I'm not. It excited me." Mindy traced a fingernail along the back of Kim's hand, fighting not to stamp her feet from anticipation like a little kid waiting for Thanksgiving dinner to be ready. She hoped she and Kim would get along well enough to have a serious relationship. If that didn't pan out, they were obviously going to have a practically torrid affair for a time, which was better than nothing.

Kim stiffened under Mindy's touch, but didn't pull away. Kim was wearing pink ankle socks. The skin between where her socks ended and her plum-colored jump suit began was tanned and silky-looking and oh-so-inviting. "I suppose you'd like to know a little about me," Mindy said. "I'm from Kentucky. I have three younger sisters. Brandi, Jennifer and Monica."

"I don't want to know anything about you," Kim said, swiping at a lipstick mark on her cup. "I thought we could talk about me. About how I feel."

"How do you feel?"

"You're so tall and beautiful," Kim blurted. She added in a whisper, "You should be a model. Or a movie star."

Mindy sat her cup down, feeling a little disappointed that Kim apparently wanted only an afternoon fling. But she was so hot-to-trot she could accept being used and forgotten this one time. She traced a finger around Kim's lips. Slowly. Kim's eyelids fluttered, her lips parted. Mindy kissed her, slipping her tongue between Kim's parted lips. She unbuttoned Kim's jump suit, pushed Kim's bra up and tickled her breasts, feeling a tremble run through a tensed body. Mindy kissed her way down the pert face, slender neck, bony chest. The red nipples were hard when she reached Kim's breasts. Kim arched her back and moaned. Mindy undid Kim's belt and slipped a hand inside her panties. Kim was soaked.

Kim pulled away all of a sudden. She jumped up and went to buttoning her jump suit. "You act like you've done this before," she said in an accusing manner, looking at her working fingers instead of at Mindy.

"Sit back down," Mindy said coaxingly, patting the couch. "I don't want to play games anymore."

"I can't." Kim looked up. Her eyes were moist, her chin trembling. "I shouldn't be here. I'm married. I have two babies at home."

"Oh," Mindy said. She usually didn't like getting involved with married women. Someone always got hurt. And it usually wasn't the married woman. But Kim was so gorgeous....

Kim snatched up her purse and bolted for the door. "Call me," Mindy begged. "If you change your mind."

"I will," Kim said. "Maybe. I don't know. I need to think." The door slammed.

"Clit-tease!" Mindy shouted. She didn't go after Kim, although she knew with a little talking and prodding she probably could've gotten her between the sheets. She didn't like talkative, hesitant sex. She wanted it to just happen. It was better that way.

Stripping off her clothes, she went to the bathroom to take a cold shower. After a moment's hesitation, she took a washcloth into the shower with her. She was about to decide all this love and relationship and feelings stuff was just a bunch of crap because she was to the point where all she wanted to do was have raw, physical sex and she wouldn't care if she even knew the woman's name.

"All work and no play makes Mindy a dull girl!" she shouted at the shower head. It didn't answer back.

*****

Two hours later, after showering and calling her family, Mindy was sitting in the deserted laundry room that was in the basement of her apartment building. It was a depressing place, with ugly green washers and dryers, and cheap plastic chairs, and lint covered floors and vending machines. Even the light fixtures were covered with lint. Didn't anyone ever clean this place? She washed her clothes, then sat watching permanent press tumble around in one dryer and towels and sheets in another.

Her emotions caught up with her unexpectedly. Pulling a tissue from her purse, she began crying quietly, thinking about her first-period talk with her sister Jenny, and her pitifully botched attempt at romance with Kim. Just thinking about all sorts of depressing things like most people do when they're so lonely and horny they can't help wondering if life is even worth the bother.

Before long, since she was in the mood to depress herself, she started thinking about how Jenny only had Mother and the girls at school to rely on in adjusting to having menstrual periods, which was like having nobody to rely on at all. Mindy couldn't help remembering how caring Mother had been when Mindy started experiencing the flowering of womanhood. Caring. What a joke. Mother had burst into the bathroom where Mindy was taking a Mr. Turtle bubble bath, carrying a razor, a can of shaving cream and a can of Right Guard. She jerked Mindy's left arm up and scraped roughly at the hair sprouting there—without saying a word.

When Mother finished, she tossed the razor and shaving cream into the bathtub, dried her hands, frowned and said, "Now do under the other arm and both your legs clear up to your crotch. Groom twice a week as long as you live in your father's house. Start using this deodorant, too. I've noticed lately you've been smelling unladylike. And don't leave the can of shaving cream sitting on the tub. You'll leave a rust ring." Mother walked out, slamming the door behind her.

Mindy sat holding the razor in one hand, covering her flowering breasts with her arm and staring at the closed door. She felt like a dog. Dogs had to be groomed, didn't they? And dogs certainly didn't smell ladylike. She wasn't even given a chance to ask 'why' or 'how' or anything.

Learning on her own, she managed to slice herself to ribbons in no time flat. She was crying and bloody and confused by the time she finished. And alone. From that day on, as the questions of approaching flowerhood sliced Mindy to ribbons, it seemed like she was only a rust ring in Mother's life.

The next stop for Mindy's self-induced depression was remembering the Wednesday evening Pastor Carling caught her hiding out behind the manse at church. She was sitting on a bench writing a love letter to an out-of-reach dream-lover identified only by the initials 'L.A.K' instead of going to Bible study class. After she delivered the letter she planned to carve a heart and her dream-lover's initials into the elm tree over yonder with a blue pocketknife she had. The only problem with the blue pocketknife was it didn't really belong to her. It belonged to a red-haired boy named Chuck and she had borrowed it from his jacket without really telling him she was borrowing it.

Along about this time, an enraged-looking Pastor Carling trotted around the corner of the manse in his bald-headed majesty. He was looking for truants, namely one Melinda Sue Brinson, who he very well knew was supposed to be in attendance at Bible study class. And so he caught her with a lustful love letter clutched in her feverish hands and a borrowed-but-not-really-borrowed pocketknife sitting beside her.

It was *so* embarrassing to get caught doing something personal when you thought you were all alone, only to suddenly find out you weren't all alone after all. Pastor Carling snatched the love letter from her hands. He practically dropped his teeth when he read it. It was filled with promises of what all Mindy Brinson would willingly stroke and what all Mindy Brinson would willingly suck if she ever had a chance to be alone with her dream-lover.

Pastor Carling pulled her by an ear into the church. He made her read her love letter to the Bible study class. Then he gave a hell-fire-and-brimstone lecture on the wages of sin to the class, using Melinda Sue Brinson as a prime example. In Mindy's wildest nightmares she couldn't picture a more horrible combination of feelings and events. It was one of the few times in her life when she sincerely believed in a Heaven and a Hell. And her squirming, stammering bottom certainly wasn't in Heaven!

What really, really irritated her, was the fact that Pastor Carling snitched on her at his earliest possible convenience and turned the love letter and borrowed-but-not-really-borrowed pocketknife over to her parents as evidence. Later that very same night, during church services, red-faced Daddy stood up in front of the entire congregation and loudly promised one sinful Melinda Sue would be severely punished, as in grounded for one month and twenty hours locked in her room reading assigned passages in her Bible followed by a 'she-better-be-perfect!' question and answer session. Daddy's public apology was the most embarrassing part of the whole situation. When church services *finally* ended and they went home, Daddy and Mother both screamed at Mindy and tried to find out just who the dickens 'L.A.K.' was. Mindy wasn't totally stupid, though, so she kept her mouth shut.

Daddy and Mother instantly doubled her punishment for refusing to talk, because that's the way they looked at things. If you did something to make them look bad, then they punished you.

Instead of being understanding when you strayed from the straight-and-narrow, they ran around making sure everyone knew it wasn't *their* fault they had a lusting, thieving trollop for a daughter. And if Daddy and Mother had known Miss Trollop was straying from the straight-and-narrow and lusting and thieving because she was practically in heat over someone with a blond ponytail and huge blue eyes named Lu Anne Kirkins, lawsy! Mindy still hated to think about what they would've done to her if they'd found out.

Along about this point, Mindy's depression really kicked in and she started doing some serious blubbering, practically baying like a hound dog on a fresh scent. Suddenly the laundry door burst open and she was once again caught doing something personal when she thought she was alone, only to all of a sudden find out she wasn't alone after all.

A slender woman with short, fluffy blond hair blew into the laundry on a gust of wind. Mindy had seen the woman once before, walking out of apartment two-fifteen at seven o'clock on a Tuesday morning, and crawl in behind the wheel of an ancient white Spitfire. With her was a top-heavy brunette bombshell who was dressed like a flight attendant. Since then, Mindy had noticed the Spitfire parked in the apartment parking lot most every night so she knew the blond woman lived in two-fifteen.

The blond woman was wearing faded jeans, a plaid lumberjack shirt and a brown coat. A green duffel bag was slung over her shoulder; a can of Budweiser was in her left hand. She hummed softly as she loaded clothes from the duffel bag into one of the washing machines without even spraying Lysol inside first. Her steps were quick and graceful as her tennis shoes moved to the machine that sold detergent.

Mindy was practically green with envy. If you were only five-seven and weighed maybe one-ten you could walk like a lady, instead of stumbling over your own size elevens every time you tried to move. The woman studied the vending machine for a few seconds, then moved back to the washing machine. She took some coins out of her purse, then returned to the vending machine.

You Light The Fire

Mindy thought that was pretty disorganized. She would have carried her purse to the vending machine and saved an extra trip. And buying little boxes of detergent from a machine was wasting money. A big box from Skaggs was more economical. The woman also put permanent press into the same washer with towels and sheets, which was plainly ignorant.

"I was hoping to be alone down here," the woman remarked. She had a husky, throaty voice that was sexy as the dickens. She ripped open a small box of Tide and dumped it into the washer. A piece of cardboard dropped into the washer along with the Tide. The woman either didn't notice or didn't care because she closed the lid and started the machine. "It's disgusting for the world to know you don't have more of a social life than washing dirty drawers on a Saturday night." The woman glanced at Mindy. "I guess you're in the same shape."

Mindy cowered behind her tissue. She needed to blow her nose, but she didn't want to do it in front of this blond sex kitten. Especially when she wasn't wearing much makeup or nice clothes and looked something less than dazzling. She tried to turn away when the woman walked over to squat in front of her.

"You crying?" The woman rested a hand on Mindy's arm. "Believe me, there's nobody worth crying over." Flitting over to the Coke machine, she energetically fed quarters into the slot. Her hands and feet were constantly moving. "Drink this," she said when she came back. "I'd give you a drink of beer, but I've slobbered in it."

Mindy lowered the tissue. "Thanks. I'll pay you back."

The woman heaved a sigh and said, "If someone with your looks is crying, there's no hope for the rest of us."

Mindy felt herself blushing. "I wish you'd stop crying," the woman said. "I get insecure when people cry around me." She plopped down in the green plastic chair next to Mindy. Her round face and blue eyes suggested she was maybe in her late-twenties. "Want to talk about it?" the woman asked.

"When I called home today my little sister, Jenny, told me...." Mindy said, dabbing at her eyes, "That she had her first period yesterday. And I'm too far away to help her." She wondered if she should be telling a total stranger about her family problems, but she needed to talk to someone. Even talking to a total stranger was better than talking to the shower head.

"Hhmmm." The woman took a sip of beer, crossed her legs and played with her shoelaces. "You're crying because you think your mom won't talk right to your sister."

"How did you know?" Mindy asked. The woman didn't talk like most of the other people in Oklahoma. She had a slight accent Mindy couldn't place.

"I've got a mom." The woman shrugged. "I'll swap her for yours. Mine goes goofy when it comes to important things like periods. She called periods *The Curse* when she talked to me. I just about shit. I thought an old mummy wrapped in white bandages was coming to sneak into my bedroom and put some kind of spell on me. I wrote a monster movie in my head called *The Curse of the Rag.* I've rewritten it since then. It's now called *The Curse of the Mom.*"

"Mother confused my sister more than anything," Mindy confided. "She told Jenny about menigrating, that's how she says menstruating, and wiggly worms and turkey basters and eggs and balloons."

The woman cracked up. When she finished laughing, she offered her hand and said, "My name's Cheerio Monroe."

Mindy laughed, then hiccupped. "I'm sorry."

"Thought that'd get a laugh out of you."

"What kind of name is Cheerio? Is it a nickname?"

"I told you my mom's goofy." Cheerio dug through her purse, then lit a cigarette. Her fingers were thin, the nails short and polished yellow. Except the thumbs. The thumbnails on each hand were scarlet red. She was wearing about twenty rings. Mindy had to fight not to stare. She'd never seen such flashy hands.

"I've got seven older brothers and sisters," Cheerio continued through a cloud of smoke. "I guess Mom was running out of names by the time I slid out, so she named me after the cereal she liked best. I'm just glad they didn't have Fruit and Fiber back then. I'd hate being named The Shits. What's your name?"

"Melinda Sue Brinson. I go by Mindy."

Cheerio puffed out a smoke ring and poked a thumb through it. "You're not from around here," she remarked. "You talk like the people at home. I'm from Athens. That's in Georgia, not Greece."

"I'm from Hopkinsville, Kentucky." Mindy stood to check her permanent press load.

"I like Kentucky," Cheerio said. "All the farms and horses. I played a concert in Lexington once. At the university."

"A concert?" Mindy laid her clothes on a table and started hanging them.

"I was a singer a million years ago," Cheerio continued, moving to the table to help fold some of the clothes. "I had a group called The Cheerios. Way back when, we had a song they played on the radio some. It was called "Everyday." Ever heard of it?"

Mindy shook her head. "I'm sorry." Her hand bumped against Cheerio's while they were both reaching for clothes. Mindy had to fight not to suck air through her teeth. Cheerio's flesh felt so warm and inviting.

The color rose in Cheerio's cheeks. She lowered her eyes, heaved a sigh and said, "I don't guess many people heard it, even back then. The Cheerios. What a goofy name. I was doing drugs when I thought that up."

"You're not a singer now?"

"Nah. Now I'm a secretary at one of the big oil refineries on the west side," Cheerio said. "You know, right across the river, where the air smells like an exhaust pipe. I roost on my ass all day. Typing. Working the telex. Shit like that. Beats starving."

"Why did you stop singing?" Mindy started folding her panties. She liked the way warm panties felt in her hands. Who needed a good-looking somebody for warmth when she had panties fresh out of the dryer to hold?

"I told you. Drugs. Heroin." Cheerio made a stabbing motion at her arm. "The needle took care of me. I'm lucky to be breathing." She laughed. She had a chuckling laugh.

Mindy took her laundry from the other dryer and started making a stack of folded towels. She couldn't help noticing Cheerio's ears were triple-pierced. A different kind of earring was in each hole. Cheerio's ears were alive with color. It was so outlandish.

"Cheerio, how old are you? You seem too young to have been a singer a million years ago."

"Just turned twenty-seven." Cheerio rubbed Mindy's pink silk blouse against her cheek. "Oooo! God, that feels good. That's what a girl was meant to feel next to her skin."

Mindy started to snatch the blouse away, but she stopped herself just in time. How rude and selfish! It was her only silk blouse, though, and she was afraid Cheerio would get makeup on it. But Cheerio was real careful with the blouse.

"You have nice clothes," Cheerio remarked. "I wore silk in the old days. Satin, too. I love satin. I was what you call a 'teen star.' God, did my parents get hot when I quit school and split to be a singer. Why I don't know. I never went to school. I just stayed home and played my guitar all day. Course, I have my G.E.D. now. I've even taken a couple of secretarial classes at the junior college downtown."

Cheerio smiled, glanced at Mindy and said, "Don't you hate educated people who lord it over everybody and act like they're better? I work for a couple of guys like that. They're ass-holes. They don't know half of what goes on at the refinery like us secretaries do."

Mindy almost got sidetracked worrying if she 'lorded' her education over everybody. She hated to get sidetracked because she'd start twisting a strand of hair around her finger and thinking. The next thing she knew her mind would be in outer space and people on Earth would be doing things to her body.

You Light The Fire

Instead of getting sidetracked, Mindy said, "Don't you ever miss it? Being a singer, I mean? It must have been terribly exciting." She frowned at a snag in her favorite pink towel. Why didn't things last forever?

"I'd be a liar if I said no." Cheerio tucked a towel under her chin and folded it. She had a dreamy look on her face. "But nothing's worth killing yourself for. I miss the actual singing the most. The travel and long hours weren't that exciting."

Mindy started loading her basket. Cheerio said, "Looks like you're finished. I guess you'll be going back to your apartment." She looked wistful. She leaned her elbows on the table and rested her chin on her hands. Her bottom swayed from side-to-side.

"I'll stay and help if you want," Mindy said, watching Cheerio's bottom swaying back and forth, feeling almost hypnotized. "It only seems fair since you helped me." As a shot-in-the-dark afterthought, she added, "I'm not doing anything tonight, anyway," in a modified version of the blatant pass.

"Don't bother," Cheerio said. "I don't fold mine. I just tote them back to my apartment and dump them in my dresser."

"Oh," Mindy said, feeling depressed again.

"What kind of work do you do?" Cheerio asked.

"I'm a high-school math teacher. I teach algebra, geometry and trigonometry. And one calculus class for advanced students."

"Mother Mary!" Cheerio clapped a hand to her forehead. "I put my foot in my mouth, didn't I? Running down educated people. I thought math teachers were old and grey-haired and wore bifocals. You can't be over twenty years old."

"My kids said the exact same thing to me on the first day of class," Mindy replied. "Actually, I'm twenty-two."

"Ah." Cheerio rubbed a thumb back and forth across her bottom lip. "Could you balance my checkbook for me sometime? You'd see then how stupid I am. How poor, too."

"Absolutely," Mindy said. "Although I seriously doubt anyone's poorer than me. Bring it over anytime. I live in apartment two-thirty." Was she rapidly approaching blatant or what?

"Okay." Cheerio hesitated before saying, "I hate you. Your legs are longer than my whole body. I've always wanted to be tall. I think you're intimidating."

"Good-bye," Mindy said, picking up her clothes and slinking out. Why would anyone be intimidated by her? She was just a person, just a woman on the prowl for what she wanted. She hated to leave, she wanted to spend more time with Cheerio, and maybe try another blatant pass or two. But she'd plainly been dismissed so what was the point in hanging around? She wondered exactly why she wanted to spend time with Cheerio since there was obviously a class difference between them. Was it lust and lust only? Or was it because she felt an unexplainable fascination for Cheerio, someone who'd lived a life so different from her own, a coarse life as opposed to a proper Baptist life.

Alone in the laundry, Cheerio softly said to herself, "I'd bet my ass you're a dyke, Ms. Mindy. I can tell by your roving, hungry eyes. God-damn, I hope I don't see you again or I'll do something stupid."

She walked to the door and watched Ms. Melinda Sue Brinson make her way across the parking lot. Mindy moved in a lithesome, loose-hipped way that made Cheerio think she'd be a great bed partner. And Mindy was sure enough a god-damn knockout, with the clearest skin Cheerio had ever seen, and giant-sized brown eyes that seemed to flow out of her face and wrap around Cheerio's heart, even after only a few minutes.

Letting herself get involved with someone as intoxicating as Mindy would be bad news for Cheerio, her ass would be in a sling and she'd never be able to get herself loose. Oh yeah, Mindy Brinson was a real heartbreaker. Cheerio wasn't interested in a knockout heartbreaker, thank you very much just the same, not after what she'd just been through with Hanna Masters. Hanna, a tall, beautiful, brunette, big-titted flight attendant.

Hanna was fun at first, no strings attached since she had a different lover in every city in her flight path. Fun, until the day she announced she loved Cheerio and wanted to settle down. But how could Cheerio settle down with a dyke who kept a lover in eight or ten different cities? She wasn't interested in settling down with any dyke, let alone a whorish one. Fuck them until it turned serious, and then hit the road, that was Cheerio Monroe's motto. Hanna swallowed a whole bottle of Seconal two days after Cheerio dumped her and was in critical condition at the hospital for a week, but eventually pulled through with only a little brain damage. It fucked Cheerio's mind. Why would anyone think she was worth dying over, even if she was a blast to be around and was a great lay, too?

CHAPTER THREE

Fall changed to winter, a trip home for Christmas was made, New Year's Day came and went, and things were certainly progressing well past the frustrating stage and rapidly approaching humorous. But Mindy wasn't laughing because she didn't see anything all that funny about having a washcloth as a lover for six months. She'd never even had a living, breathing lover for as long as six months.

She was on her back in the middle of the living room floor, twisting a strand of hair around a finger, resting her feet on the couch and ignoring the stack of algebra tests on the coffee table she needed to grade. "Kim," she said into her phone, since she was wasting time on a clit-tease. "I suppose it's possible you could've all of a sudden metamorphosed into an aspiring bisexual when you turned thirty. I don't know much about such things. Why don't you go to the library and check out a book?"

Kim giggled, no doubt feeling deliciously wicked to be engaging in mental masturbation with her *lesbian friend*. Mindy said, "What you're talking about isn't scary to me. I adore women. I even dream about women."

"Do you dream about me?" Kim asked, sounding even more deliciously wicked.

"Why would I?" Mindy asked, not caring about the scorn in her voice.

"Tell me what it's like with a woman," Kim whispered. Her breathing got heavier. She was probably poking a hand between her legs and fiddling with her own trigger.

"I'll pass," Mindy said, thinking about Cheerio Monroe. She'd seen Cheerio four times around the apartment complex since they met in the laundry. Cheerio made a U-turn all four times and sped the other direction, making Mindy feel like chucking a rock at her or something. Maybe pulling out a rope and lassoing the evasive wench.

Mindy got up and wandered into the kitchen for a diet Coke. She opened it, leaned against the refrigerator, closed her eyes and pictured Cheerio's round face and bright blue eyes. She doubted she was in love with Cheerio, not after one twenty minute meeting in a laundry. But maybe she *was* in love since she was an easy touch when it came to blonds, and Cheerio *had* been on her mind almost nonstop since that night in the laundry. She was definitely in lust, as base as that seemed, because she couldn't force from her mind the memory of how inviting Cheerio's skin had felt when their hands bumped in the laundry.

"Where do you work?" Kim asked.

"I don't," Mindy said. "I'm independently wealthy."

"Is it something you'd get fired from if they found out about you?" Kim asked, sounding practically breathless. "You people have exciting lifestyles. You're like enemy spies, always on the edge of danger, never knowing when something will go wrong and you'll lose everything."

"Invite me over for dinner so I can meet your husband," Mindy said, scratching a calf with a big toe.

"Frank would *kill* me." Kim sounded uncomfortable all of a sudden. She giggled and said, "He's taking me to the horse races at Hot Springs, Arkansas this weekend. I love going to the races. He lets me bet as much as I want."

"Wow." Mindy wandered to the living room window and looked out. The parking lot below was nearly deserted. It usually was on the weekends. Cheerio's car was in the parking lot, though, parked beside some bushes. Mindy had spent so much time looking at Cheerio's car the last few weeks she had Cheerio's license number memorized. But no way was she crawling to Cheerio's apartment to grovel. She had some pride, after all, and considering the way Cheerio had summarily dismissed her in the laundry that night, it seemed like it was up to Cheerio to make the first move.

"Do you know any places where lesbians go to get lucky?" Mindy asked more or less hopefully.

"Of course not!" Kim blurted. A toddler squalled in the background. "I have to go."

"Don't call me again. I don't see any purpose in talking to you."

"I'll call again," Kim said. The game-playing witch added in a whisper, "I love you."

"Give me a break!" Mindy shouted. She slammed the phone down. It rang almost immediately.

"Melinda Sue?" a man's voice asked.

"Yes?"

"This is Terry Belk. The computer science teacher from school? I was sitting around thinking about you, I can't get you out of my mind. How'd you like to go out? Dinner or a movie or whatever?"

"I'm sorry," Mindy said, rolling her eyes. Both the twentyish men teachers at school hit on her practically every other second. Why couldn't there be a twentyish woman at school who was hot for her instead of only a bunch of middle-aged married women? "I have a date tonight. I was just leaving. I don't date people I work with, anyway."

*****

Mindy picked up the phone book and absentmindedly flipped through the pages, wondering if she should just start with the A's and call everyone in town until she found a lover. She felt practically giddy when she finally pulled her head out of her rear

and thought to look for a gay information line. She approached
ecstasy when she found a gay information line listed. Her bubble
popped about three seconds later when she called and got a
recording. A recording was even more worthless than a soapy
washcloth or a married woman who enjoyed borderline-obscene
phone calls while refusing to do anything.

She slammed the phone down and decided to go driving
around. Someplace. Anyplace. No place. Anything beat sitting
around her apartment again on yet another lonely Friday night.
Maybe, if she was lucky, she'd have a wreck and that would give
her a chance to ask the other driver, "Do you happen to know of a
place where lesbians go to hang out? If I don't find a lover soon, or
at least find someone to spend a romantic evening with, I'm going
to go totally insane. Come on. Give me a break. I'm looking at a
fairly small possible-sex-partner-pool here. All I need is for someone
to point me in the right direction and I'll take over from there."

She put on her slinkiest dress, a red sleeveless chemise with
brass-tone grommets, and red hose and black heels and maybe a
ton-and-a-half of makeup and perfume. When she got down to her
Mustang she couldn't help noticing she had a flat tire, which
certainly made her day. She felt so fortunate to have gotten all
dolled-up to go no place and then find out all she would really get
to do was change a flat tire and get all sweaty and smelly. Stomping
back to her apartment, she changed into a baggy sweat shirt and
jeans, feeling practically petulant the whole time.

The tire-changing was accomplished with no problem, but
then, when she was letting the jack down, the tire tool jumped
unexpectedly and practically amputated her left hand. "Ouch!" she
bellowed, staggering to the curb with her left hand squeezed
between her knees. When she got to the curb, she plopped down to
examine her practically amputated left hand. She didn't even have
a scratch, but her knuckles were sore as the dickens where the tire
tool had bopped her.

It was about this time she noticed Cheerio clumping down the
steps, wearing a black miniskirt with the hem clear up to there, and

carrying a beer can in her left hand. She swivel-hipped to her antique white Spitfire, fished her keys out of her purse and tried to unlock her door. She dropped her keys, and bent to pick them up. She dropped them again. She muttered, "Fuck it," drained her beer and tossed the can into the bushes before picking up her keys again.

Mindy felt practically disgusted because she didn't like litterbugs. She didn't think saying the F-word made a woman especially attractive, either, not unless it was said in bed. Cheerio glanced at Mindy, her eyes widened, she sped toward the stairs. Mindy looked around for a rock, wondering if she could brain Cheerio from thirty feet away. Not hurt her, just slow her down enough so she could be captured.

Cheerio stopped speeding away all of a sudden and stared at Mindy, who was staring at Cheerio. After a few seconds of bilateral staring, Cheerio swivel-hipped over, leaned against Mindy's fender and asked, "What are you doing?" She crossed her legs at the ankles, with an agonizingly sexy husking of her hose. Her legs were absolutely heavenly. Mindy hoped she wouldn't start drooling all over herself. Why was she always dressed like a ragamuffin every time she saw Cheerio?

"Well?" Cheerio asked, burrowing in her purse before lighting a cigarette.

Mindy took her drool-covered knuckles out of her mouth. "Trying to amputate my left hand," she grumbled.

"I was thinking about going out," Cheerio said. "But I guess I'm too drunk to drive anywhere if I can't hold onto my car keys."

Mindy sucked on her knuckles some more. Did she see an outline of nipples under Cheerio's rose-colored top or what? "Are you okay?" Cheerio asked.

Mindy heaved a sigh and mumbled, "I suppose," through a mouthful of knuckles. She wanted to yell: *No, I'm not okay! I'm almost to the point where I practically climax every time I take a step! If you really want to know what I'm doing then I'll tell you. I'm sitting here scheming about how to get you naked because I'm almost positive you're a lesbian, but you won't respond to my passes and it irritates the dickens out of me. Maybe I should just throw you down and rip your clothes off with my teeth! Would that intimidate you?*

"Ah," Cheerio said. She puffed out a smoke ring and poked a thumb through it.

Mindy leaned down and picked up a twig so she'd have something to occupy her hands. Well, actually, she was trying to look up Cheerio's skirt but who cared? "You never did bring your checkbook over so I could see how poor you are," she pouted.

"I didn't think you were serious." Cheerio shrugged.

"I said I'd balance it for you," Mindy practically snapped because she was not in what you'd call a real good mood, considering her current lustful condition. "Are you calling me a liar? I'm not a liar."

"Mother Mary!" Cheerio exclaimed, looking more or less irritated. "Don't get your panties in a wad. Is your hand hurt bad?"

"No. I'm only pouting."

"Ah," Cheerio said, locking eyes with Mindy, losing herself in the brown depths of Mindy's eyes despite her best intentions. She watched Mindy sucking on her knuckles, full-lipped mouth working industriously, and pictured how Mindy's mouth would feel on her body. "Are you hungry?"

"I'm starved."

"I was afraid of that," Cheerio groaned. God-damn her for her weakness, but she *had* to have Mindy Brinson and piss on the consequences. "There's an Italian joint about half a mile from here," she surrendered, pointing to the west. "Do you want to have dinner? My treat."

Mindy's head bobbed. "I'll change," she said quickly, like she was afraid Cheerio would change her mind. Mindy thundered up the stairs two steps at a time, all legs and elbows and bouncing tits and flying brown hair. Two seconds later she came thundering back down, wearing a clinging red dress that knocked Cheerio for a loop.

"I'm amazed at the way my knuckles quit hurting all of a sudden," Mindy chattered as they got in Cheerio's car.

"Huh?" Cheerio babbled, losing touch with what was happening, her eyes drifting up Mindy's legs. *Intoxicated.* It was her own fault, she knew what would happen if she got too close to the fire and damned if she wasn't going to get burned. Hell, she was going to get worse than burned. She was going to get roasted *alive.* She could already feel the flames coming.

*****

The 'Italian joint' was a dimly-lit place called Perlozzo's. It was a nice restaurant, with red carpeting and paneled walls and small round tables covered with white cloths and empty wine bottles for candle holders. To Mindy, it was romantic as all get out. Cheerio seemed to know everybody who worked there. Mindy supposed so, anyway, because Cheerio swapped barbs with everybody and they were given the best table, the one way back in a corner beside a forest of potted plants.

Mindy practically dropped her teeth when they got to the table and Cheerio held her chair while she sat down. She was more impressed when Cheerio didn't look embarrassed, even though several other diners were launching frowns in their direction.

"Thank you," Mindy murmured.

"No problem," Cheerio said, spreading her napkin on her lap. "Someone as classy as you deserves to be treated good."

Cheerio ordered chicken Parmesan. Mindy had the clams and linguine. They shared a carafe of wine. Cheerio kept bumping knees and feet under the table during dinner. She also kept reaching out to touch Mindy's hand and remark how nice Mindy's dress was or how pretty Mindy's hair looked in candlelight. During the touches, Cheerio's eyes shone and her hand always lingered longer than was really necessary, sometimes for as long as a minute at a time.

Mindy felt practically dizzy the whole time. She hadn't been seduced in such a grand manner in forever. It didn't take long for her to decide it sure was a lot of fun sitting at a corner table, eating clams and linguine, sipping wine, looking across a flickering candle at a sexy blond nymph and chatting about clothes and jobs and families, instead of stupid stuff like metamorphosing bisexuals.

After dinner, Cheerio invited Mindy to her apartment. The inside of the apartment smelled like jasmine incense and cigarette smoke. It was furnished with lots of flowers and a yellow phone with a red cord and a psychedelic peace sign poster thumbtacked above the fireplace. And a framed picture of Lyndon B. Johnson with an orange dart stuck in his nose that Mindy couldn't help gawking at. A yellow bra and three pairs of hose draped across the ceiling fan also caused her to gawk.

"Act like you own the place," Cheerio said casually. She walked over to Mindy, enveloped in the same heavenly perfume Mindy had smelled in the car; it smelled like Wind Song. She quickly brushed her lips against Mindy's cheek and then disappeared into the kitchen.

Mindy noticed a small wire cage sitting on the floor, so being a naturally snoopy person, she walked over and looked inside. A white gerbil was in the cage. "Hi, Ms. Gerbil," she said, poking a finger inside the cage.

The little beast lunged and tried to bite her. She heard its teeth click together. The gerbil jumped on its wheel and started spinning around like crazy. "You hateful thing," Mindy hissed. "I'm tempted to pinch your head off!" She didn't like animals that bit.

Cheerio came back carrying two cans of beer. She laughed and said, "I see you've met Hard-on. He's about a million years old so he's kinda grumpy. Did he bite you? He bites everyone but me. I won't feed him if he bites me and he knows it."

"No, but he sure tried to." Mindy looked at Cheerio. "Did I hear right? His name is...?"

"Hard-on." Cheerio held out a beer.

"Thanks." Mindy opened the beer and took a sip. What a funny name for a gerbil. If she had a gerbil named that, she wouldn't even be able to talk to it because she couldn't say that word. "Why did you name your gerbil that?"

"He's a guy," Cheerio said with a shrug, as if that was explanation enough.

"Did you know you have a yellow bra hanging on your ceiling fan?" Mindy asked. Cheerio was obviously a relaxed housekeeper. She wasn't a slob, but she wasn't obsessive-compulsive, either. Mindy liked that.

"Think blue would look better?" Cheerio asked, glancing at the bra as she tossed a stack of newspapers from the couch onto the floor. "I need to take my trash out one of these days."

"I don't know," Mindy said. Actually, she thought a ceiling fan looked best without any bra at all hanging on it. She sat on the couch where the newspapers had been, and crossed her legs, making sure her hem jumped to the moon. But her size eleven shoe went 'clunk' on the coffee table and she felt clumsy instead of seductive.

Cheerio moved to a stack of records beside the Marantz stereo, squatted and flipped through them. She shifted a little sideways as she flipped, giving Mindy a clear look up her skirt, casting Mindy a sideways glance to see what response she got, and practically causing Mindy to suck on her knuckles some more. Cheerio was a definite beanpole blond with huge blue eyes and a one hundred percent full and round bottom. Yum-yum! And the way the muscles on the tops of her thighs tightened when she squatted...lawsy!

"You have a nice apartment," Mindy said.

"Thanks. See? I'm not a liar, either. This is the song I was telling you about the other night." Cheerio sat on the couch, rested a hand on Mindy's thigh and handed over a forty-five. "Everyday," by The Cheerios was printed on the record. Beneath the title was printed: C. Monroe and C. Czuprynski.

"You wrote the song, too?" Mindy asked.

"I wrote the lyrics." Cheerio nodded then glanced away.

"You're the most famous person I've ever known. I can't picture what it's like to actually have people pay to hear you sing." Mindy examined the record. "Who's C. See-zoo-prinski?"

Cheerio smiled. Her eyes had a dreamy look. Or a sad look. Like she was remembering something she didn't want to but wanted to all at the same time. "It's pronounced Cha-prin-ski," she said. "Capulet Cha-prin-ski. Her mom was a Romeo and Juliet fan. I called her Cappie. We wrote the music together."

"Where is she now? Did you two breakup?" Mindy asked, thinking: *Please say you did. If you're attached and you only want me for an hour or two of cheating fun I'll probably throw myself under a bus because I can't take it anymore. I want so much more than that from life. I want everything life has to offer a woman and that doesn't leave much room for one-night stands.*

Cheerio looked at her hands. Her eyes went from half-dreamy half-sad to all-sad. She licked her lips and said, "Cappie died a long time ago."

"I'm so sorry. I shouldn't have been nosy," Mindy said, feeling as guilty as a hound dog caught in a hen house with eggshell on its face.

"Don't feel bad." Cheerio shrugged. "I've learned to handle it. Kinda." Her eyes looked into Mindy's, then moved away. She tugged at a loose thread in her couch.

"I'm listening," Mindy said.

"We overdosed one night in New York," Cheerio said. "That's why I said I was lucky to be breathing the other night. I pulled through. Cappie didn't make it."

"Oh, how horrible!" Mindy felt like slapping herself. What an understatement!

Cheerio crossed her legs, causing her hem to jump to the vicinity of her eyebrows. She ran a thumb up-and-down her beer can and scratched her thigh, making the requisite sexy husking sound on her hose and practically catapulting Mindy through the roof. Cheerio finally said, "Did I tell you me and Cappie signed on as the opening concert act for a big-name group one time?"

"Really?"

"We thought we had it knocked," Cheerio said dreamily, "and that we'd hit the big-time. Didn't last long. I got doped-up one night in Milwaukee and missed a show. They fired us the next day." She took a sip of beer and studied the bra on her ceiling fan. "I don't mean to bug you with my past," she said after a moment. "That's not what you're after."

"I don't mind. Talk to me about anything you like." Mindy put an arm around Cheerio. Not rushing things but because Cheerio looked so pitiful. She felt frail and delicate, like a piece of fine china.

"It got goofy after Milwaukee," Cheerio said, resting her head on Mindy's shoulder, tickling Mindy's thigh. "We went back to New York to record our second album, but I couldn't handle it. I was sticking some large dollars into my arm by that time, and so was Cappie. Everyone in the band was. There was so much riding on us. So much pressure." She laughed without sounding amused. "Everybody was on us all the time. The record company. The mother-fuckers. It's hard to be creative when that many people are hassling you. It was a gang-bang. Me and Cappie were the ones on our backs." She paused to sip her beer. "One day I woke up in the hospital. I was hurting bad. When they told me Cappie was gone, I wanted to die, too."

Mindy didn't say anything. She kissed the top of Cheerio's head. "I'm sorry," Cheerio said. "I had a rotten day before dinner with you." She sat quietly for a long time, drinking her beer. The gerbil's wheel went squeak-squeak. Mindy finally asked, "May I listen to your record?"

"Not when I'm around," Cheerio said. "I can't listen to my old songs. Especially 'Everyday.' It's about my oldest brother. He was a Marine, and got killed in Vietnam. They gave Mom a medal. She would rather have had Alvin back."

"You make me feel ashamed," Mindy said. "You've been through so much, with people dying and all. Compared to you, I've had a life worrying about things that are stupid next to life and death worries. I feel like such a little girl."

"I was a little girl back then," Cheerio said softly. "I threw everything away. A four-octave soprano. A great band." She cleared her throat and continued, "I haven't sung since Cappie died. I hum sometimes, but that's it. I walked away from it after she died. After I got out of the hospital." She stood, wandered to the stereo and turned it on. A Joan Baez song was playing.

"Do you still use drugs?" Mindy wondered aloud.

"Nah," Cheerio said. "I did six months in detox and a couple of years in therapy after Cappie died. Her death scared me too much to mess with the stuff again. Cigarettes, beer on the weekends and cussing are the only vices I have now." She chuckled, flashing her eyes at Mindy. "And women."

"Women are an understandable vice," Mindy agreed.

"What would you like to do?" Cheerio asked. "We can polish our nails. I've got about thirty colors you can use. I've depressed you enough. God knows I've depressed myself enough."

"We can do whatever you want."

Cheerio walked to the couch. She straddled Mindy's legs and plopped down in Mindy's lap, sending her hem over her hips. Her arms snaked around Mindy's neck. Mindy ran her hands up-and-down Cheerio's thighs. Cheerio nuzzled Mindy's throat and murmured, "Let's fuck our brains out and not worry about anything else."

"That's fine with me," Mindy said.

"This is how my relationships usually go," Cheerio whispered. "I fall madly in love with a woman after five minutes, and then spend the next six months joined at the hip with her, suctioning the life out of her, and then spend a year breaking up with her."

"I don't care for that," Mindy said. Taking Cheerio's face in both her hands, she brushed her lips against Cheerio's, then slipped her tongue into Cheerio's mouth when Cheerio's lips parted. Cheerio's mouth tasted like peach lip-gloss and cigarettes and beer. Cheerio kept her eyes open during the kiss, her dainty, colorful hands fluttering over Mindy's eyes, cheeks, chin.

Mindy slipped her hands under Cheerio's top, promptly lost her balance, tumbled not-so-gracefully off the couch onto the floor and 'whooshed' out half of her breath when Cheerio landed on top of her. A few writhing seconds later they were both more or less naked.

"Let's go to bed," Cheerio panted.

"Later," Mindy practically panted herself. She stretched out beside Cheerio and turned into a lips-hands-and-fingernails maniac, feeling like a starving lioness with a fifty percent kill ratio gorging herself on a freshly-downed antelope while it was still kicking as she licked, kissed and tickled her way down Cheerio's body.

"I've never had a lover as pretty as you," Cheerio whispered. "Can't we go to bed? I want to take my time with you."

"Ssshhh," Mindy whispered back. She poked her face between Cheerio's thighs, opened the door to Cheerio's insides with her tongue, female insides all steamy and liquid, and savored the silky warmth with her mouth. She felt like dying the whole time because Cheerio tasted so good. Lots better than clams and linguine, even.

Cheerio grabbed a major league orgasm, coiling her legs around Mindy's head, pulling Mindy's hair, sobbing/crying, thrashing around on the floor. Mindy practically chortled because she adored noisy lovers, mostly because she was one herself. As Cheerio soon found out.

In the shower afterwards, during the hair-washing and curious exploring of a new body with soapy washcloths, Mindy said, "I hope you don't have plans for the weekend. I'm going to keep you busy until Monday morning."

"I've got to work tomorrow."

"But it's Saturday," Mindy whined, feeling more or less crushed.

"I need all the overtime I can get," Cheerio said, gnawing Mindy's shoulder. "I get off at five. We can go out tomorrow night."

"Why don't you come to my apartment? I'll fix us dinner and we can do what comes natural." Mindy tried to pull Cheerio to the bottom of the bathtub, but there wasn't enough room, Cheerio was pretty tall even if she was a runt, and they got all tangled up in arms and legs. They oozed through the shower curtain and landed on the bathroom floor with a soggy 'plop.' The situation suited Mindy just fine so she locked her knees into Cheerio's hips and grabbed a double-handful of luscious bottom.

"Shit," Cheerio groaned. "Am I ever going to get you into bed?"

"We're heading that way," Mindy replied. "We'll be there before morning. I don't mind staying up all night. I don't have to work tomorrow."

"Bitch," Cheerio hissed.

"You talk too much," Mindy said, poking her tongue into Cheerio's mouth.

CHAPTER 4

"I won't get hurt at this place you're taking me, will I?" Mindy asked, frowning skeptically. "I've never been inside a bar is why I'm wondering." She added, "Oops," because she shifted to second gear and gave her Mustang too much gas and the tires barked.

Cheerio looked at her like she was strange or something. She propped a hi-top tennis shoe on the dash. Mindy wasn't sure she cared for that, but she didn't say anything. She just hoped Cheerio hadn't stepped in chewing gum or something.

Smiling, Cheerio ran a hand up-and-down Mindy's thigh in a familiar way, like lovers do after they've been sleeping together for three and a half months. Mindy smiled back and squeezed Cheerio's knee with the same kind of familiarity.

"Shit!" Cheerio gasped, as Mindy all of a sudden changed lanes to avoid colliding with a man in a red Corvette who whipped in front of them. "Be careful in this part of town. All the cops know this is a gay section and they love to give us tickets."

Mindy didn't answer. She was watching the road too closely. Tulsa traffic still bothered her. Especially when she came to a confusing intersection that had six lanes on each side, with so many lanes going left, so many right and so many straight ahead. She was always afraid she'd choose the wrong lane and get swept away to who knew where until she was totally lost and spent all her money on gas trying to get back, and finally starved to death on the side of the road and no one ever heard from her again.

"That's not it, is it?" she asked, wrinkling her nose when she saw a flashing sign that said: Hot, Hard And Horny. It didn't sound like the kind of place she'd like to spend a Saturday evening in May.

Cheerio cracked up, shook her head no, and pointed to a building past the flashing sign. The Eager Beaver was a big brick building with a gravel parking lot and double glass doors. Painted on the glass doors was a picture of an erect beaver in a pink dress and pigtails. The beaver was rubbing her paws together and leering. Inside the glass doors were wooden swinging doors like you'd see in an old cowboy movie. Inside the wooden doors was the smell of cigarette smoke and stale beer. The walls were painted white, the carpet was brown. A mahogany bar stood against the far wall, and a woman wiped the bar with a towel, between serving drinks. The juke box played a rock-and-roll song above the sound of clacking pool balls, the sound of the clacking balls bringing back memories of Corrine.

About eighty brown tables with chairs covered in black vinyl were scattered around the room. The dance floor with spinning red, yellow and blue lights was in the darkest corner of the building, complete with a gyrating couple frantically groping each other. A wooden stage with musical equipment occupied another corner. Hanging above the stage was a huge white banner with pink lettering. The lettering said:

Appearing Tonight
Oklahoma's Own
SILKY WET

Only about fifty women were sitting at the tables, but it was still pretty early to party, or so Cheerio claimed. About a third of the women were what Mindy would call hard-core, dressed in tight jeans with chain belts and cowboy boots and leather stud watchbands and white tee shirts with the sleeves rolled up to expose tattoos. They were sexy as the dickens in a blatantly erotic way, and several of them winked at Mindy. She smiled back. She'd never said she wasn't an outrageous flirt! She practically felt prideful looking at the women because not only did they seem hot for her, but also because here it was 1975 and women had come far enough that they could dress like men in public.

Cheerio and Mindy helped themselves to bar stools. Wine glasses hung from a wooden rack over the bar. A red beer clock, its hands indicating 9:30, and dozens of different-colored bottles sat behind the bar.

The bartender, a towel draped over her shoulder, smiled at Cheerio and Mindy as she laid napkins in front of them that said: You Shouldn't Drink and Drive...So Don't Drive.

"Well, well, if it isn't Miss Cheerio Monroe," she boomed in a deep voice. "Haven't seen you in some time. Must be five or six months."

"Hi, Sherry," Cheerio replied to the bartender. "I've been busy."

"Looks like," Sherry said, shooting a meaningful glance in Mindy's direction. Cheerio rolled her eyes and smiled mysteriously. Sherry asked, "Where's Hanna?"

"Who?" Cheerio squeaked, flinching like she'd been hit, pretending to be wide-eyed and innocent.

"Ah," Sherry said. "Draft beer?"

"You bet," Cheerio said. "It's been a long week."

Sherry plunked a frosty mug down in front of Cheerio, glancing at Mindy again as she did. Her glance was more or less brazen. "Who's Miss August?" she practically cooed.

"Mindy Brinson," Cheerio said. "Mindy, this is Sherry Johnston."

"Hi, there." Mindy offered her hand.

"Hi, there, yourself." Sherry whistled. "Better watch this one, Cheerio. Every stud-ette in here'll be trying to get in her pants. What'll it be, Miss Mindy?"

"May I have a low calorie beer?"

"Don't worry about watching your figure. I'll keep an eye on it for you." Sherry winked as she plunked a bottle of beer on the bar.

Mindy didn't say anything. She'd noticed Sherry watching her figure. She put a five dollar bill on the bar. Sherry said, "Put that stuff away. I'll run a tab."

"Stop flirting and get to work, Sherry," a tiny waitress in jeans and a white apron, standing at the opposite end of the bar called.

"Hi, Cindy," Cheerio said, waving at the waitress.

"Hi, yourself, Cheerio. What's shaking?"

"Nothing but your chest."

Cindy popped her chewing gum. "I inherited these from my dad," she drawled. "He's got the biggest tits in Creek County." She glanced at her breasts, which were somewhere in the neighborhood of enormous.

Sherry fixed three drinks, then strolled back from the waitress station and leaned her elbows on the bar. "Have you two decided to drag me into the stockroom yet?" she purred.

Cheerio laughed. "You horny old goat! What if we said yes? You'd run as fast as you could go."

"Try me." Sherry wiggled her eyebrows.

"Every dyke I've known who talks a good game is a lousy lay." Cheerio looked at Mindy. "What do you think?"

Mindy peeled a piece of paper from her beer bottle, and didn't answer. What Cheerio said was more than a little true, although Mindy wasn't going to confess any knowledge of such a thing in public.

"Do I hear sarcasm?" Sherry cupped a hand behind an ear. She leaned forward, checked the bar in both directions as if making sure no one could hear, then cleared her throat. "Let's discuss you, Cheerio," she said. "How big is yours? Does your new lover know they call you The Bottomless Pit?"

With that last comment, Mindy choked on her beer, sending a stream of foam down her chin and onto her pink turtleneck. She snatched up a napkin and wiped beer from between her breasts.

Cheerio laughed. Sherry, with a knowing nod, said, "I remember my first beer." She moved down the bar to a woman wearing a St. Louis baseball cap. "What'll it be, doll? How about those Cardinals? Think they'll win it all this year?"

"Is she mad at you?" Mindy asked, worrying Cheerio had insulted Sherry by saying she was a lousy lay.

"She loves being a horse's ass," Cheerio snorted, swiveling her stool around. "Some decent-looking gals in here. Too bad I've got morals. Being a slut would be a blast." She snapped her fingers and swayed on her stool. "I feel like dancing." She grabbed Mindy's arm. "Look! There's a girl over there with the cutest ass in the world. Think I'll see if she wants to dance." She looked at Mindy. "Will you get jealous? Are you the possessive type?"

Mindy didn't say anything. She started to peel at her beer bottle some more, but Sherry walked up and swept away her bottle. "Ready for another?" Sherry asked.

"May I have a martini?" Mindy asked with a flirtatious smile. She had no idea what was in a martini but she'd seen people on TV drink them. "With a little olive stuck on a toothpick?"

"I think I get the point," Cheerio remarked.

"Wet or dry?" Sherry asked.

"Wet," Mindy said, taking a shot in the dark and trying to appear confident. She felt the weight of Cheerio's eyes.

"You know," Cheerio said, running a thumb across her bottom lip and putting on her thoughtful expression. "When you kind of arch your eyebrows and get that look on your face that says you know everything and the rest of the world is full of dumb-asses, it pisses me off. I've seen that look at least a thousand times in the last three months."

"Three and a half months," Mindy said, arching her eyebrows higher for Cheerio's benefit. She watched Sherry dump some stuff into a tall glass and stir it with a long spoon. Cheerio said, "What have I done, god-damn it? Really? Have I done anything so major that you want to start a fight?"

"I thought you were going to dance," Mindy said breezily. "I'm sure I heard you mention something about a great bottom." She peered into the glass Sherry set down in front of her.

"Ah," Cheerio understood, and tapped her beer mug on the bar.

Mindy stirred her martini with the olive stuck on a toothpick. She decided it didn't look all that good. Not as good as a chocolate milk shake. Cheerio said, "So I won't dance. Mother Mary! Are you always this big a bitch?"

Mindy arched her eyebrows even higher, wondering how Cheerio would look with a fist stuck in her mouth. She couldn't say she was particularly enjoying her first visit to a bar, not when it was obvious Cheerio had roving eyes and Mindy had a jealous streak a mile wide. She wished they were at home, curled on the couch, eating popcorn and watching TV.

"Hi, Jo," Cheerio said, her voice friendly, like everything was just great in the world and she wasn't a millisecond away from getting her eyes clawed out by a certain jealous bitch.

A fortyish woman with short brown hair and green eyes and two chins came through a door behind the bar. A tall, languid-looking brunette was with her. The brunette moved to the other end of the bar, cocked an ear toward two waitresses, and started whipping out drinks, looking like she had as many hands as a centipede.

"Haven't seen you in a while, Cheerio," Jo, the fortyish woman with two chins, said, tying a white apron around her waist.

Sherry pecked Jo on the cheek, slapped her bottom, and said, "Hi, hon. You're late."

"Tammie's car wouldn't start," Jo said, nodding toward the languid-looking brunette. She started washing glasses. "Good turn out tonight," and swept her eyes around the bar. "I hope the Fire Marshall doesn't pay us a surprise visit."

"You and me both," Sherry grimaced.

Mindy looked over her shoulder. The crowd had expanded to well over two hundred women all of a sudden, with more boisterous women pouring through the swinging doors, everyone exchanging greetings and kisses, except for two women who made a beeline for each other and started exchanging punches and kicks and shrieking about a woman named Denise. A bunch of jeering spectators separated the two combatants and shoved them to opposite sides of the bar. The place was noisier than a high school basketball game.

"That's why I sit at the bar," Cheerio said. "You get to hear all the shoptalk. Jo, your two-faced wife's been hitting on us every five seconds."

"She's cheap." Jo laughed. "Knew it when we got married. One of her ex's told me." She shot Mindy a look and practically cooed, "Who's this lovely vision?"

"I'm getting pissed," Cheerio complained, looking playful instead of angry. "No one's said *I'm* pretty. I don't come here to get treated this way." She folded her arms across her pale blue sweater and pretended to pout.

Jo and Sherry chorused, "You're pretty, Cheerio," in-between popping caps off beer bottles a mile a minute and sloshing alcohol into glasses. There was a steady stream of waitresses going to and coming from the waitress station. The place was definitely hopping.

Cheerio laughed. "That's more like it! This is Mindy Brinson. Mindy, this is Jo."

"Glad to know you, Mindy." Jo dried her hands on a towel before offering one. "Any friend of Cheerio's is a friend here."

"Hi, Jo." Mindy shook hands.

"We don't get enough pretty young girls in here," Jo said. "You know how it is. Pretty young girls bring the older ones with the dollars. You and Cheerio sit there and let the ladies think they can hit on you. Don't worry about your tab."

"I wouldn't feel right drinking for free," Mindy said.

"Bull-shit," Jo replied. She turned away to answer the phone. Someone at the other end of the bar bellowed, "If that's my husband tell him I'm not here!"

Everyone hooted. Mindy looked to see if it was Kim bellowing about her husband. It wasn't. It was a nasty-looking red-head.

"Am I still getting the eyebrow treatment?" Cheerio asked. Mindy didn't say anything. She forced down another sip of martini. She had already learned two things about wet martinis. One, they went straight to her head. Two, they didn't taste as good as chocolate milk shakes.

Cheerio crawled onto her stool and balanced herself on one foot. Everyone was pointing at her and laughing. Mindy begged, "Please don't do that. It's embarrassing to me."

"So you can talk!" Cheerio said, her eyes wide in amazement. "Are you drunk or something?"

"Nah," Cheerio said. "But it's early yet." She gave Mindy a narrow-eyed look and hissed, "Who's this Kim bitch who called you last Sunday morning when you were sleeping in my arms? How often does she call you?"

"Just a friend. I told her to quit calling last time I talked to her because I have a lover now and don't have time for her." Mindy gave Cheerio a narrow-eyed look and hissed, "And just how many women in this place have you slept with?"

Cheerio rolled her eyes before cupping her hands around her mouth and shouting, "I want all the little girls in here to know I can drink 'em all under the table! You bunch of wimp-ettes! There's not a real dyke in the whole bunch! I'm a better dyke than all of you put together!"

Most of the women gave Cheerio the finger. The rest laughed. Mindy hid her face in a napkin. Cheerio hopped to the floor, landing gracefully in her hi-top sneakers and clapped Mindy on the shoulder, saying, "Sherry! Bring this lady a rum and Coke. She's a real lady. She needs a lady's drink."

Mindy tried to protest. She'd already had a beer and two-thirds of a martini, which was about a beer and two-thirds of a martini over her limit. Nobody listened, though. Before she knew it, a glass was sitting in front of her. She started to scold Cheerio when she was distracted by a drawling voice. "What about you, Cheerio Monroe?" the drawling voice asked. "Are you a lady?"

"Alysa Leigh, is that you?" Cheerio squealed, swiveling her stool around. "If I'd known you were around, I wouldn't have said I was the best dyke here. You're more of a dyke than I'll ever be."

Alysa Leigh was maybe the most striking woman Mindy had ever seen. She was about twenty-nine years old, had chalky-white skin, a long thin nose, and was tall and skinny, maybe five-ten by one-thirty. Her jet-black hair was stunning—long, teased into disarray, tied with a pink ribbon that ran down her back to her waist. Her dark eyes peered out from behind thick black mascara that was pulled into a point somewhere in the vicinity of her ears, and eye shadow that reached to her hairline. She was knuckle-sucking alluring in black leather pants, a white velvet blouse cut clear down to there, and black stiletto heels.

Alysa grabbed an empty stool and sat facing them. She focused a pair of taunting eyes on Mindy, tickled Mindy's chin and said, "Cheerio Monroe, you hit the jackpot if you're getting horizontal with this body. I'm jealous as hell." She traced a finger between Mindy's breasts and exclaimed, "Nice tits! I bet they're sweet-tasting. Can she walk and chew gum? Something this breathtaking has to be dumb as a dustpan."

"Mooo," Mindy lowed, deciding she felt exactly like a roast sitting in the meat department at Skaggs, being judged for too much fat and so forth. She felt like telling Alysa about her college degree and how she was a secondary-certified mathematician and all that impressive stuff. She didn't have time to say anything because Alysa lunged for her crotch. She managed to slap Alysa's hand right before it got personal as the dickens.

Cheerio laughed and said, "When did you get back in town?" She lay a hand on Alysa's knee. "Last I heard, Silky Wet was on the road."

"I'm here to say we've been on the road." Alysa stopped groping Mindy and started fluffing her hair on her shoulders, looking egotistical as all get out. "Five months worth. We hit Texas,

46

You Light The Fire

Mississippi, Alabama, Georgia, Florida, Tennessee, Louisiana and every unknown, unnamed place between here and there. Best time was in New Orleans. We signed on for eight weeks at this cozy place near Bourbon Street. We ate every kind of gumbo and seafood 'til it was coming out of our ears. It was great, but it's nice to be home."

"Fractured a few groupie hearts, I bet," Cheerio said.

"I remember talking politics with a girlish tail or two." Alysa grinned lasciviously. "You going to sing with us tonight?"

"Haven't found a singer yet?" Cheerio crossed her legs as she lit a cigarette.

"Hell, no." Alysa looked disgusted. "Right now we're tossing a coin. Loser has to sing." She stole Cheerio's cigarette. "We took a girl with us on this last trip but she didn't work out," Alysa continued. "Had her mind on her clit instead of what she was doing. Talk. That girl talked and talked. If she wasn't wrapping her legs around someone, she was talking. We gave her a bus ticket when we got to Jackson, Miss." Her face turned serious. "We keep hoping you'll join up with us, Cheerio."

"You doing so good you need a secretary?"

"Damn it, Cheerio." Alysa slapped her thighs. "You're holding us back. With you up front, we'd be ready to make some serious money. We'll give you forty percent of the gross."

"No way." Cheerio shook her head.

"Forty-five?"

Cheerio pinched Alysa's cheek. "It's not the money, honey," she explained. "If I went back to singing, it'd be 'good-bye, Cheerio.' I'd run to drugs like a starving horse to oats and all your gross wouldn't be enough to stop me."

Alysa looked disgusted again. "You going to be scared of dying the rest of your life?" she asked. "I promise to thump anyone who gets near you with dope."

"Going to thump yourself?" Cheerio flicked her lighter and held it to Alysa's face. "Look at those eyes. Been doing coke?

Maybe smoking a little marijuana? I shouldn't be talking to you. You want something I don't have—self-control."

"Get that damn thing away before you blow me up," Alysa muttered, pushing at Cheerio's hand. "If I thought you'd get hurt, I wouldn't ask. Think about it, Cheerio. With that soprano of yours, we'd kick New York's ass. Bright lights. All the money and girlish tail you want or need. How can you say no?"

Cheerio laughed. "I clear eight hundred a month at my nice, safe, secure job," she said. "It's not much but I never worry I'll wake up half-dead in a hospital."

Alysa squeezed Cheerio's knee and cajoled, "I'm saying I want us to go away and make a million dollars and be famous and live happy ever after. I love you, Cheerio."

Cheerio took a turn at looking disgusted. Mindy took a turn at feeling practically fire-breathing green at the thought of someone trying to steal her lover right in front of her. What kind of woman did everyone think she was, some kind of floozie who'd let someone just sashay up and waltz away with her lover in broad bar-light?

"Leave her alone!" Mindy hissed, hackles raised and claws extended. "No means no. Maybe she really does want to sing, but your band isn't good enough for her." She all of a sudden shut up when she noticed how Cheerio and Alysa were staring at her like she was from outer space. She decided rum and Coke could sure embarrass a person.

Alysa's eyes flashed, her nostrils flared. She tossed her head and made a kissing sound in the general direction of Mindy's crotch. "Don't get pissed at me, sugar tail," she sneered. "You'll bust my heart. Cheerio don't need no bosomy bodyguard. How'd you like to climb outta your Levi's and wrap them mile-long legs around my face? I'll give you the best tongue-lashing in the free world."

"You're easily the rudest woman I've ever met," Mindy replied icily. She added, "Bitch," more or less under her breath. She knew she should have been insulted. But Alysa was so girlishly cocky it was hard to get mad at her—so long as she limited her propositions to women Mindy wasn't in love with.

You Light The Fire

"Don't sit there blushing at me," Alysa taunted. "You started it."

"It's okay, Mindy," Cheerio said. "Me and Alysa go way back. If we didn't argue about me singing, we wouldn't have much to say to each other."

"You'll perform for me someday, Cheerio," Alysa sneered, making a kissing sound in the general direction of Cheerio's crotch. "You'll sing for sure the day I nail your bouncy little ass to the wall. Are you a real blond? Or a fake like everyone says?"

"She's no fa..." Mindy began, her voice trailing off before she finished because she didn't think it was anyone's business that Cheerio was definitely a true blond.

"I'll never sing for you, ass-hole," Cheerio insisted. "On-stage or in bed." She looked at Mindy. "Remember what this bitch said. When she comes sniffing around trying to find out what color your bush is, remember how she is. Talking girls into bed is what she lives for."

Alysa laughed. Right before she reached out a hand and traced a finger around Mindy's left nipple. Cheerio slapped Alysa's hand away and said, "I don't appreciate you pawing my main squeeze."

"Chill, Cheerio," Alysa replied, holding both her hands in the air. "With the mouth *that* one's got, she don't need no bodyguard, either. She's near as mouthy as you. I'm the one who needs a bodyguard sitting here with you two clit-cracking sugar boogers." She squeezed Mindy's knee, tried to run a hand up her leg and purred, "Let's you and me go somewhere and see who can make the other grab the brass ring ten times the fastest."

Cheerio flipped cigarette ashes in Alysa's hair. Mindy said prissily, "Keep your hands where they belong, please." She pinched Alysa's arm and gave her a dirty look. Alysa grinned, slipped off her stool and ruffled Cheerio's hair. Cheerio gave her a dirty look, too.

Alysa looked at Mindy and airily said, "Wait until you see me on-stage, Miss Knockers. You'll be nothing but another groupie,

49

crawling after me on your hands and knees at closing time, saying you love me in the morning because I'm a great fuck, picking me apart in the afternoon when you see I'm not perfect, breaking my heart in the evening when I come home and find you in bed with someone else. Why did you treat me like that, Miss Knockers? I loved you with everything I had. I'd always thought we were so good together, right up to the end when you left me."

"Now *that's* cynical irony," Cheerio said. "Or is it smart-ass bull-shit?"

Alysa sauntered away, holding a hand above her head and twirling a finger in the air. Four other women in the bar with leather pants and teased hair broke off conversations and followed her to the stage. Fifteen or twenty zillion other women gathered around the stage, smiling toothy smiles and wiggling their breasts at Alysa and the others.

"Is she always like that?" Mindy asked. "She acts like every woman in the world wants her."

"If she goes home alone it's because she wants to," Cheerio answered. "Alysa Leigh is only her stage name, by the way. Real name's Mary Smith."

"I think it's time we quit wasting money on rent for two apartments," Mindy said.

"Huh?" Cheerio blurted, in confused disbelief.

"I'll get some boxes and move my stuff to your apartment tomorrow." Mindy slipped an arm around Cheerio's waist. "It won't take but a few hours. I don't have much. I'm all but living at your place, anyway. Most of my clothes are there already."

"God-damn," Cheerio said. "Footloose one second and shacked up the next. Just that quick." She snapped her fingers.

"If you want to dance you can dance with me," Mindy said. "Or are you ashamed for everyone to know I'm yours?"

Cheerio leaned over and stuck her draft beer-tasting tongue in Mindy's mouth. Most all the women around the bar whooped and applauded. Sherry and Jo started humming T*he Wedding March.*

"I asked if you were the possessive type," Cheerio said. "All you had to do was say yes."

"I'm not possessive. Not too much, anyway."

Cheerio cracked up. She grabbed Mindy's hand and led the way to the dance floor. Mindy sighed happily because she was head-over-heels in love with the most beautiful lover she'd ever had. And the most worldly and confident, too. And the most mentally stimulating and exciting to be around. And definitely the most talented in bed.

She had more than she'd ever hoped to find in a woman.

"God-damn me for my stupidity," Cheerio whispered. "But I've fallen in love with you and I can't do anything about it." She pushed Mindy to one of the few open spaces along the dance floor wall, where kissing, groping couples were lined up in the semi-darkness. She kissed Mindy, running her hands under Mindy's sweater to cup her breasts at the same time. And Mindy let her without protesting, even when Cheerio unzipped her jeans and slid a hand into her panties and touched her. She just closed her eyes and wrapped her arms around Cheerio's neck and accepted the groping as the public display of ownership it was intended to be.

CHAPTER 5

"How's Mindy doing?" Mom asked.

"She's fine," Cheerio said. She was sprawled on the couch, watching Billie Jean King kick the shit out of a nobody French player in a Saturday afternoon Wimbledon match. "She's at the library with a teacher friend she met at a symposium. They're working on an algebra presentation or something to use when school starts this fall."

"I think the world of her," Mom said. "When you two came here in April I had the best time with her."

"Yeah," Cheerio grunted. Mindy and Mom had been almost inseparable during the April visit to Athens, putting their heads together and chattering about recipes and housecleaning tips and other interesting shit like Cheerio-manipulating strategies. Cheerio guessed Mindy was the kind of daughter Mom had always wanted.

"How are things between you two?" Mom asked. "You've been with her longer than any other woman that I can remember." Mom worked hard at being *The Good Parent Of A Lesbian*, trying to use all the right words and everything.

"I'm still god-damn goofy over her," Cheerio admitted. "Even after three years."

"She's the best thing that ever happened to you," Mom said softly. "I used to agonize over you constantly, the way you'd jump from one woman to another. I knew you were searching for something you could never find, and I knew how you suffered over each break-up. You're as sensitive and caring as any person I know, even if you like to act like a loudmouth drunk sometimes."

"Fuck you, Mom," Cheerio said, laughing.

"Is that any way to talk to your mother?" Mom asked, laughing, too. "Seriously, I'm glad you have Mindy. If you ever do anything to ruin what you have with her, I'll take you over my knee."

"Talk to you later. I love you."

"I love you, too," Mom said.

Mindy and her teacher friend came through the door, successful, determined looks on their faces, chattering about the quadratic equation or something, their arms loaded with papers and books. They piled the shit on the coffee table and went into the kitchen to make some iced tea. Alma Karr was about a hundred and ten years old and wore bifocals about a foot thick. She was definitely the classic grandmother type and Cheerio guessed that's why Alma and Mindy got along. Mindy had a talent for bringing out the grandmother instincts in people.

Pleasant. That's what shacking up with Mindy was. It was pleasant waking up naked with the leggy filly in the morning and seeing her start smiling as soon as her eyes opened. It was pleasant cozying up on the couch with her to watch TV and eat popcorn and listen to the bull-shit artistic interpretations she gave to everything she watched. It was sure enough god-damn pleasant fucking her, she was creative and uninhibited in bed. It was pleasant to say, "I'm going out with my friends to raise hell," and have her say, "Okay, I'll see you when you get back, I have some tests to grade, anyway," instead of whining to tag along. Cheerio guessed the pleasantness was why she was still with Mindy, even though things had grown well beyond the serious stage.

Someone knocked on the door. It was Donetta, the straight black newlywed from three doors down. She was wearing big oven mitts and holding a smoking pan in both her hands. Tears were rolling down her cheeks. Cheerio pointed to the kitchen. Donetta raced that way, bawling, "Mindy, my souffle fell and I don't know why! I did everything you told me to!"

"Oh, lawsy!" Mindy sympathized. "How embarrassing for you!"

The phone rang. Cheerio heard Alysa's familiar voice. "God-dammit all to hell!" Alysa cursed. "I've got our books fucked-up and the stone-cold bitches in the band are accusing me of felony embezzlement. Damned if I know where I went wrong. Does Mindy have time to look at things if I come over?"

"Come ahead," Cheerio said. She sat down to watch the rest of the Martina Navratilova semi-finals match. Pleasant. If you liked living in the middle of a crisis center. But none of the problems were major so it was laughable more than anything.

Oh yeah, Cheerio Monroe was snared hook-line-and-sinker, so far gone she couldn't imagine life without Mindy, and the feeling was...pleasant. Cheerio guessed she could handle things. She didn't see how her relationship with Mindy could get any more serious. It was kinda like swimming. The first time you did it you were scared as hell of the water. But once you jumped in and went for it, you found out it wasn't really scary, and it was even fun once you learned how to do it well.

*****

The alarm clock buzzed. Cheerio, one eye squeezed shut and the other a slit, reached over and slapped at it groggily. "Good Monday morning, Cheerio Monroe!" Mindy said brightly. The greeting was followed by a kiss and a squeeze on a sleek thigh and a quickie attack session.

"Are you finished with me?" Cheerio panted afterwards.

"You may go," Mindy said, waving a hand in dismissal. Cheerio staggered into the bathroom to shower and get ready for work.

During breakfast, Cheerio said, "What's with you? You have me when we go to bed, you wake me up around three to have me, and you have me again first thing in the morning."

Mindy poked a foot under the table and between Cheerio's knees and mournfully said, "I know. The honeymoon must be over if we're only making love three times a day."

Cheerio threw a piece of toast at her and grumbled, "Slut."

"I'm not a slut," Mindy said, popping the piece of toast into her mouth. "I'm a vibrant young woman with a healthy sexual appetite."

Cheerio rolled her eyes and said, "If you snag my hose with your toenails you're dead."

Once Cheerio was sent out the door, Mindy dressed and drove to the local mall and dawdled from store to store, being nosy and tightfisted. As she dawdled, she pretended to herself she was a happy young housewife, which she pretty much was during the summer, with a lover who wore expensive dresses, or even a hard hat, to work. While she was dawdling and pretending she really was who she really was, she also pretended to herself she was planning how perfect everything would be for her lover when she came home from work, which was pretty much the truth in real life, too. She didn't know why she pretended to herself that she really was who she really was. She just did.

She laughed on the inside every time she saw an elderly couple out walking who motioned to her and chattered between themselves when they saw her dawdling along, clutching her little sacks filled with important things like a container of fresh-ground pepper or a bottle of nail polish for Cheerio because she knew they imagined her as a happy young housewife with a virile, handsome husband at home.

Thinking about how people looked at other people and invented all kinds of imaginary lives for them sometimes reminded Mindy of a blond lover named Vicki she'd had in college. Vicki had been older, thirty-six, respected in the community, and a member of the Daughters of the Confederacy. She had also been married with three children.

Vicki and Mindy met while standing in line at the grocery store, fell madly in love at first sight and carried on a practically torrid affair for six months. Vicki was Mindy's first mature lover, the one who made her feel truly comfortable with her own sexuality. Things all of a sudden changed one night when Vicki's husband, who was supposed to be out of town on business, quite unexpectedly kicked in the door of the secret apartment Vicki kept and caught his wife in a filmy red negligee and wide-eyed Melinda Sue Brinson naked on the couch, except for the pillow she was clutching to her breasts and the TV Guide she grabbed for her crotch.

The husband, with bulging eyes, said, "I thought you were having an affair with a man. How can I deal with this? Boy-oh-boy, that's a good-looking girl." Vicki said, "Tom, why don't you shove your bulging eyes up your rear end and get out. Before you go, I want you to know you're only so-so in bed."

A messy divorce followed and Vicki lost custody of her three children. Terrified, Mindy received a subpoena, but was spared from appearing when Vicki stood up in court, openly admitted everything and told the judge he could kiss her ass if he didn't think she could provide a good home for her children. Soon after, Vicki moved to San Francisco because she said she was sick to death of living in a place where people imagined pretend lives for other people to satisfy their own idea of *perfect*, instead of accepting people for who they really were. Mindy had been heartbroken. She cried practically nonstop for six months when Vicki moved to San Francisco, because Mindy had to stay behind with her family, since she was only nineteen and in the middle of her sophomore year at Berea College. She hadn't seen Vicki since, although they still exchanged Christmas cards.

After Mindy finished dawdling through the mall, she drove home and went swimming, then lounged by the pool listening to her transistor radio and getting trembly-chinned knuckle-sucking teary-eyed over her latest paperback lesbian romance. Mindy lounged by the pool to read even though she didn't like sunbathing. But Cheerio had mentioned at least a zillion times that she preferred lovers with good tans and spent a lot of time working on her own tan. About three o'clock Mindy showered before giving the whole apartment a good cleaning. At four-thirty she started their evening meal so it would be waiting on the table when Cheerio sashayed through the door at five-thirty. But Cheerio didn't get home until six-thirty.

"You ruined my lamb chops, eggplant casserole and green beans almandine," Mindy snapped. "I'm borderline furious in case you're wondering. I should think at your age you'd know how to use a telephone. I was starting to worry you'd been mashed on the expressway." Mindy wasn't really borderline furious. She was just throwing the kind of fit she saw women on TV throw when their mate came home late for dinner without calling. And so what if she was maybe wanting her relationship to resemble a *model* heterosexual relationship? Why shouldn't she have *a model lesbian* relationship? Why shouldn't every lesbian strive for a relationship she considered *model*?

"Suck bat-shit," Cheerio said, looking very cross. "I'm tired of people at work using me. I have to put up with those ass-holes, but I don't have to put up with a god-damn goofy gash-ette whining about lamb beans or whatever the hell you're saying."

"If you feel a need to converse in such an anal-retentive, guttersnipe manner, the socially accepted word for bat-doo is guano," Mindy said, throwing a potholder at Cheerio. "You never fight fair because you cuss like a sailor. I refuse to respond in an equally coarse manner."

"Tough-titty," Cheerio barked.

"I'm serious," Mindy said. "Your foul mouth makes me feel like stomping you sometimes."

Cheerio threw her purse to the floor. "Jump and get it, stork-legs!" she shouted. "I'll slap a hair-lip on you long enough to comb!"

"Stork-legs!" Mindy shrieked, feeling murderous. "That irritates the piss out of me! My next-door neighbor called me that when I was ten. I picked up a rock and nailed the little bastard in the head and knocked him off his bike!"

"Hah!" Cheerio retorted. She jumped up-and-down and wagged a finger. "Look at that red face. Look at that frown. You are human. You can lose your temper and cuss and get down in the gutter with the rest of us. I finally broke down the Miss Calm-And-Always-In-Control front you put on for everybody! You like to pretend you're perfect, but I've got news for you, sweet pea, you're not!"

The people next-door pounded on the wall, meaning you-know-who and the blond witch were making too much noise. Cheerio pounded back. "Fuck you, ass-holes!" she shouted.

"I want a house," Mindy said. "I'm sick of this place."

"Huh?" Cheerio's chin dropped to the floor. "Huh?" she repeated, dumbly.

"I want to buy a house," Mindy said. "You and me. Us. We have a stable, lasting relationship. Anybody with half a mind can see that, so why shouldn't we have our own home?"

Cheerio bolted like a colt on gelding day, out the door, leaving it hanging open, and thumped down the stairs. Mindy went out on the landing and stood watching with her mouth hanging open. Cheerio zoomed across the parking lot, past the dumpsters and around the corner of the building. Mindy was already wearing her running shoes so she threw her legs in gear and galloped after Cheerio.

Cheerio ran along Fifty-eighth Street, past the K-Mart, past the Safeway, across Princeton Avenue against the light and almost getting run over, past the barbecue place and the Skaggs and the Zales Jewelers. In front of the movie theater she looked over her shoulder. Mindy was gaining on her like a thoroughbred would on a plow mule. Cheerio started hopping on one foot so she could pull off a heel. Then she hopped on the other foot and jerked off her other heel. She tossed her heels into a nearby bush and took off running again.

Mindy felt humiliated because everyone driving by was pointing and laughing at them. Since they were already making public spectacles of themselves, Mindy cupped her hands around her mouth and roared, "You can run from me, Cheerio Monroe, but you can't hide!"

Cheerio slowed. She veered off the sidewalk, across a patch of grass and toward a Salvation Army collection spot in front of the Otasco Store. There was a tired-looking green couch, a chipped coffee table and a floor lamp at the collection spot. Cheerio plopped down on the tired-looking green couch.

She was still sprawled on it when Mindy arrived. Cheerio's head was between her knees, she was heaving and gasping. "Why did you stop?" Mindy jeered. "I was just getting warmed-up." She pranced around with her hands on her hips, shaking her feet and flexing her calf muscles.

Cheerio hawked an oyster between her knees, sounding like a six-foot redneck truck driver. "Mother Mary," she groaned. "I've got to quit smoking. I can't run for diddly anymore." She kicked her feet onto the coffee table. The feet of her hose were in shreds from running on pavement, her hem was clear up to her bottom, sweat was beaded on her forehead and upper lip.

"I doubt you tried to run away because we had a fight," Mindy said. "That's not like you."

Cheerio shook her head. She sucked in a big gulp of air and pressed a hand to her chest. "I didn't mean what I said. I had a bad day."

"Are we through skirting the issue then?"

Cheerio rubbed her eyes. "A house," she moaned. "God-damn, Mindy. A house. A thirty-year mortgage. That's a...a...it's a mind-fucking concept is what it is."

"No," Mindy corrected. "It's a commitment. I realize that. What I want to know is do you think you'll someday find someone you love more than me? Someone who loves you more than I do?

I've found the woman I want for the rest of my life, and I'm willing to make a house commitment for her. Are you?"

Cheerio squirmed on the couch. She stared into the distance. She chewed on a fingernail and studied the traffic going by. Finally, she muttered, "Roasted *alive*." She stood and took Mindy's hand. "Let's go home."

After a shower, dinner at the golden arches, and getting ready for bed, Cheerio said, "Where will we get the money? Have you thought about that? Who'll loan us money? Can dykes get house loans?"

"We'll find the money. I swear we will."

*****

"Cheerio and I want to buy a house," Mindy stated matter-of-factly into the phone. "We need help. We can get a loan for most of it, but we want to borrow some from you and Mother. Fifteen thousand. That's for the down payment and closing costs and a few pieces of furniture and other miscellaneous stuff."

The phone was quiet.

"Daddy, maybe I should tell you something before you make a decision," Mindy offered. "Something I've wanted to tell you for a long time."

"Melinda Sue," Daddy said, sounding tired. "You don't have to tell me anything. You're my daughter and I love you. But I still wish other things for you. Better things. You're living contrary to God's way."

"Maybe your God, but not ours," Mindy said. "Is religion going to cloud your decision?"

Daddy heaved a sigh. "Is this what you want? Is Cheerio what you want?"

"Yes. Most definitely."

"I want the deed to the house to be in your name only," Daddy said. "And I want it mailed to me."

Mindy gave Daddy a long-distance finger. "No deal. The deed will be in Cheerio's name and my name. It's *our* house, after all."

"Seventy-five hundred," Daddy said, in his let's-make-a-deal tone of voice. "That's all I can hide from your mother."

"Will you co-sign the bank loan for us if we have any problems?"

"I'll do whatever it takes," Daddy said. "But you have to promise to never tell your mother or sisters what you tried to tell me. It would put them all in the grave."

Mindy chatted some more before hanging up. As soon as she put the phone down she started to call Daddy back and tell him to stuff his money. She felt like he was buying her silence. She finally decided to let it ride. A house was worth practically any price. How could she have a *model* relationship without a house? And she'd been silently hiding what she was for so many years. Did it matter now that she was an adult?

*****

Mindy fell in love with the fourteenth house they toured, a beige brick house with two red elms in the front yard and a wooden privacy fence around the backyard, and a Bermuda grass lawn that Mindy sneered at. Bermuda grass was considered a weed in Kentucky, although it was popular in Oklahoma because of the hotter, drier climate.

The inside of the house was carpeted in a cozy brown, except for the kitchen and bathrooms, which had beige linoleum. "It needs painting on the inside," Cheerio said smugly. Mindy grumblingly conceded the walls used to be white but were kind of yellowish now.

"But," she said brightly, "I for one know how to operate a paintbrush. It's not all that complicated." She walked into the kitchen and drooled over the butcher-block counters and almond appliances, and gas stove like any real cook cherished. Leaving the kitchen, she strolled into the great room, with Cheerio trailing behind her, and gawked at the vaulted ceiling with an imitation wood beam running down the center, and the fireplace, and the ceiling fan.

"I love it," Mindy said, running a hand across the oak mantel. "It feels like home."

Cheerio put on a toothy smile that said 'bite my bottom.' "We can't afford it," she practically chortled. "Sixty-two five is too much for our budget."

"We'll just see about that." Mindy told the realtor to offer fifty-five thousand even, and wrote a five hundred dollar check for "earnest money."

"I'll make the offer, but don't expect anything," the realtor said.

Mindy pooh-poohed. "Oklahoma is a depressed housing market right now," she said confidently. "I bet these people have maybe lost their jobs because of the oil industry slowdown and will jump at any offer."

Cheerio hit the vaulted ceiling. "Do you hear what you're saying?" she shouted. "I work for the depressed oil industry. What if I lose my job? I almost got hit by the last bunch of layoffs."

Mindy laughed, knowing full well experienced executive secretaries were a valuable commodity. Cheerio said, "You're cold-blooded. Taking advantage of people when they've maybe lost their jobs and everything, and then laughing about it."

"I'm not cold-blooded! They have something to sell. I made an offer to buy it. If they don't like it, all they have to do is refuse and we'll go on looking."

"Hah!" Cheerio sneered. "Looking for another house? Or looking for someone else to try and take advantage of?"

"I want a house," Mindy said, fighting to control her temper. "I'll manipulate the system any way I can to get what I want. I for one won't have trouble sleeping at night." Cheerio stuck her hands in her pockets and went out to the car. She was mumbling to herself and scuffing at the Bermuda grass with every step.

You Light The Fire

*****

The Saturday they moved was hectic as the dickens. Cheerio went around with her lips pouted and a cross look on her face, bitching about everything. "I've lived in this apartment for ten years," she grumbled. "I'm not sure I want to leave. Maybe I'll stay here. You ask why? Because I hate change, god-dammit!"

Mindy heaved a sigh and went back to running around like a chicken with her head cut off. She was ready to plop Cheerio and Hard-on both into the dumpster to get hauled away with the rest of the garbage. Hard-on was bitching as much as Cheerio. He got all excited and ran around his cage flinging litter everywhere, then he ran around his wheel, then he went back to flinging litter.

Sherry and Jo came over in the morning to help carry the heavy stuff down to the U-Haul. They were the only ones worth a damn, what with grunting and sweating and laughing and shoving on things they were at least trying. Alysa came wafting in at midday, dressed in one of her patented white/black velvet/leather outfits and stiletto heels and sunglasses. She was toting a cardboard bucket of honey-dipped fried chicken and a twelve-pack of Bud Light. She looked like a TV commercial.

"I hope you two are happy," she snapped as soon as she hit the door. "I had to set my god-damn alarm to haul my ass out of bed this early. Jesus H. Christ, but noon is an ungodly hour for a human being to be awake."

"What are you wearing?" Cheerio bellowed as soon as she saw Alysa. "You can't help in those clothes."

Alysa took off her sunglasses. Her eyes looked like ten miles of bad road. "How gauche!" she declared. "I'm not here to work. I'm in charge of refreshments and supervision." She held out her chicken and beer as proof.

"You can haul your ass out of here if you're not going to work, Mary Smith!" Cheerio roared.

Alysa's eyes flashed, her nostrils flared. She tossed her head. "Well, just go fuck yourself, Cheerio Monroe!" she shouted. "And don't call me Mary Smith. I don't answer to that name."

"I agree with Cheerio," Mindy said. "None of us has the time or patience for spectators."

"Well, just go fuck yourself, too, Miss Knockers," Alysa sniffed. She plopped her cardboard bucket of honey-dipped fried chicken and twelve-pack of Bud Light on the floor, spun on a stiletto heel and headed toward the door with one hand on a hip and the other twirling her sunglasses.

"Where are you going?" Cheerio asked.

"Home to change clothes," Alysa answered. "I won't be excluded from a day as special as this. Not even by the devil's own hangover and two domestic-type hens with peevish attitudes."

Cheerio followed Alysa to the door. "Wear work clothes!" Cheerio shouted. "Real work clothes. Not frilly stuff for working on your back. Mary Smith!" Alysa gave Cheerio the finger over her shoulder and kept walking.

Alysa was back thirty minutes later, wearing jeans and cowboy boots and a black mesh top and no bra. Her nipples could be seen from clear over yonder. Everyone jeered her but she pitched in and worked like a real trooper, even if she did keep mumbling, "If any of you tells anyone that the great and famous Alysa Leigh, the greatest female guitar player in the world, actually stooped to manual labor, I'll kick the shit out of you. That's a promise, not a threat."

Mindy was already exhausted by the time the U-Haul was loaded and they drove to the house and met the truck from the furniture store with their new light blue and grey couch and matching chair and ottoman and brand-new almond Whirlpool washer and dryer. She was running on empty by the time they moved all the boxes from the truck to the house and took the wrapping off the furniture and hooked up the washer and dryer and said hello to two snoopy neighbors.

Right off the bat, Cheerio found something in the house that was broken. The drain under the kitchen sink was leaking. Cheerio promptly went on a rampage. She bellowed profanity at the drain. Then she stomped into a bathroom, flushed the toilet and bellowed something about how it was a good thing the toilet worked right or she'd throw it out in the front yard and plant geraniums in it. Marching into a bedroom, she bellowed even more profanity about the five thousand boxes sitting on the bed so there was no place to sleep, fuck or fight. And she continued to rant and rave about houses and lovers and gerbils and mortgages and God's warped sense of humor in general and life in particular, for some time.

During Cheerio's rampage, everyone else stood in the kitchen like little mice with wide eyes, studying the leaking drain under the sink and feeling too terrified to breathe. Jo finally whispered, "What's got her in such a tizzy? A leaky drain is nothing. Put a pan under it and it's fixed."

"I don't know." Mindy shrugged. "She hasn't let me touch her in weeks." Everyone frowned. Mindy said, "I think she's just all excited about the house and commitments. I'll take her a beer and calm her down."

"You're braver than I am," Alysa said. Sherry and Jo nodded sympathetically.

Mindy girded her loins and tip-toed into the master bedroom. Cheerio was sitting on the floor under the window, with her back against the wall. She was tossing orange darts at the poster of Lyndon B. Johnson she'd hand-carried from the apartment.

"Hi, there," Mindy squeaked, what with being a terrified mouse and all. She handed Cheerio the beer.

Cheerio sucked down about half of the beer in one swallow. She burped like a six-foot sailor and asked, "What name goes on the mailbox?"

"Monroe and Brinson," Mindy said sweetly. "I already bought the stick-on letters."

"It'll take us years to get all this crap sorted out." Cheerio flung another dart at Lyndon Johnson.

"No, it won't." Mindy eased down beside Cheerio. "I'll work and slave and have everything neat and orderly by next week. It'll feel like home in no time."

Cheerio heaved a sigh. "Are you happy now?"

"For the time being. Until another scheme pops into my head." Mindy squeezed Cheerio's thigh. "I bet your outlook improves once all the boxes are unpacked and things put away. We'll buy a glider to put on the patio. A lawn mower. A few new lamps and pictures. Flowers for the box outside the great room window. That's about all we can get for now before we run short on money. I don't mind because, the way I figure things, if we buy and fix and furnish all at once it won't leave us anything to do over the years."

Cheerio promptly walked out. She just as promptly got into another 'who's the biggest witch' contest with Alysa in the kitchen for putting a bowl under the leaky drain. Alysa snapped, "Get outta my face, Cheerio Monroe. I'm only trying to help."

Cheerio countered with, "I've been hearing rumors the dyke you're running with this week is into handcuffs and riding crops."

Alysa meowed, "Grow some eyebrows."

Cheerio retorted, "You've got a flat ass, and your mama sleeps with guys."

Alysa sniffed, "That hurts, that really hurts, no-tits."

Sherry and Jo both yelled, "That's enough!"

Mindy took a turn at heaving a sigh about the time Alysa shouted, "I don't know why Mindy puts up with you! You're doing your best to ruin a special day!"

Cheerio retorted with, "She's no day at the beach to live with, either!"

Alysa barked, "Who cares? With her tits and ass and face she could be Attila the Hun and it wouldn't matter."

Cheerio cackled, "Go play with your handcuffs, Mary Smith."

Alysa stomped into the master bedroom and announced, "I'm leaving. My feelings have been slammed enough for one day."

Mindy asked her to stay. Alysa tossed her head and said, "If you're not getting any loving from that dyke, you should unload her. She's one stone-cold bitch," and stomped out.

Hearing the front door slam a few seconds later, Mindy started clearing boxes off the bed so Cheerio would have a place to sleep, fuck and fight. For some strange reason Mindy had a feeling Cheerio was more in the mood for the latter, though, and less interested in the other two.

In the kitchen, Cheerio took a fresh beer and a honey-dipped drumstick from the refrigerator, and went to the backyard, next to the privacy fence, and sat cross-legged on the grass to eat and drink and philosophize about a lover named Michelle she'd had one time. Michelle had owned fifteen cats. Sure enough, Cheerio Monroe liked cats as much as the next dyke, but fifteen cats was just too many. But loving Michelle meant loving her fifteen cats, even if it gave you a serious pain in the ass stepping on a cat every time you took a step. The cats were the baggage you had to accept when loving Michelle.

Mindy's baggage was her house, and her five hundred dollar a month mortgage payment, and her dreams, most of all. Dreams that she'd fulfill come hell or high water because, even with all her cute, girlish ways, the dyke had a spine of stainless steel and nobody could stop her when she got a head of steam. Cheerio knew she'd learn to carry Mindy's baggage eventually. But she couldn't make the adjustment overnight without digging her heels in just a little, and it pissed her off that everyone expected her to give in without a good fight.

*****

The first thing Mindy noticed when she got home from school on Monday, a week after they'd moved, was a certain blue-eyed blond witch in the great room wearing darling white coveralls with crotch-level cuffs. The witch was humming and painting the walls salmon and apparently operating a paintbrush just fine, although she always claimed she didn't know how to operate one.

Mindy wasn't totally stupid, so she kept her mouth shut. She changed clothes and sat at the kitchen table to work on lesson plans, acting like she didn't even notice the blond witch in her darling white coveralls with crotch-level cuffs. She also pretended not to notice she was practically drowning in her own drool every time she looked at a certain blue-eyed witch she was pretending not to notice.

During dinner, homemade sloppy joes instead of red goop from a can, Cheerio, with lowered eyes and impassive face, mumbled, by way of explanation, "I got caught up on my work so I left the refinery early today. Things are kinda slow now. Orders for gasoline are way down."

"Uh-huh," Mindy said. "Pass the potato chips, please."

On Tuesday when Mindy got home from school, she noticed a blond woman who looked an awful lot like Cheerio Renee Monroe perched on the roof sweeping leaves out of the gutters and cleaning bird droppings off the chimney. Later, she noticed the same blond woman raking leaves and hosing down the driveway and chatting gaily with the elderly couple who lived down the street and always came by at the same time each day walking their cocker spaniel.

During dinner, Cheerio, with lowered eyes and impassive face, mumbled, "I took a few hours of vacation this afternoon."

Mindy said only, "Uh-huh. Pass the tomatoes, please," even though she wanted to scream because Cheerio's tee shirt was damp from the driveway-hosing-down and her breasts were outlined and her nipples were practically poking Mindy in the left eye.

On Wednesday when Mindy got home from school, she discovered Cheerio under the kitchen sink. Wrenches and plumbing fixtures and a home repair manual were scattered all over the floor. Mindy walked over and poked her face under the kitchen sink.

Cheerio had a sheepish look on her face. "I didn't go to work at all today," she mumbled. "I'm taking the rest of the week off, and I'm going to fix this drain if it kills me."

"Uh-huh," Mindy said. She walked to the refrigerator for a diet Coke. She opened it, turned around and said, "I can't keep still any longer. You blond-haired, blue-eyed bitch! Pardon my French, but that's what you are."

Cheerio mumbled something incoherent. Mindy said, "All this week I've felt like you were ready to call us quits just because I wanted a house. Is trying to build a stable home for us such a hateful concept to you? I can't believe that's true, even if you did balk and drag your feet and bellow profanity every step of the way in getting here. I think, if the truth be known, you love our house as much as I do."

Cheerio lowered her face and brushed some invisible lint from her blouse. "Are you through chewing on me?" she asked.

"Not yet," Mindy said in her teacher voice. "If you don't change your attitude, I don't know what I'm going to do. Maybe throw you out in the front yard and plant geraniums in you."

"You're right. I've been a horse's ass." Cheerio cleared her throat and took a deep breath. "I want to have a commitment ceremony a week from this Sunday afternoon. We'll invite everyone we know and have it in the backyard. I know a gay priest who'll come over and say a few things. Then I want to say some things to you in front of everybody, things I've been meaning to say for a long time."

Mindy burst into tears. "Yes," she said triumphantly. "I'll marry you." After she finished crying, she asked, "So why have you been acting so terrible?"

"Fear of swimming," Cheerio mumbled, her face flushing.

CHAPTER 6

"I'm sure glad tomorrow is Saturday," Mindy remarked. "I can use some time off. Mid-term tests and grading all the papers wear me out." She was rocking slowly in the glider. Her arms were wrapped around her for warmth. She pretended not to notice the goose bumps on her arms because she wasn't ready to go inside yet. April nights were nice, but they sure had a knack for adding a bite to the air along about sunset.

Cheerio was sitting on the ground, watching a pile of leaves burn like it was the most interesting sight in the world. Mindy didn't really approve of what Cheerio was doing because the burning would leave a brown spot on the grass. Besides, it was probably illegal. It made Cheerio happy, though, so Mindy didn't nag.

Cheerio glanced up. "Uh-oh," she groaned.

"Hhmmm?"

"You have that look on your face," Cheerio said. "The spacy one that means you're going to start babbling about the meaning of life or something."

"I've decided the backyard looks empty," Mindy said. "Not really empty, though. More like it's not as full as it should be. Or could be."

"You want more lawn furniture? You want to plant a tree?"

"I want us to have a baby," Mindy quietly announced. A baby was all she needed to complete the *model* relationship she dreamed of having. They'd been in their house for nine months and that situation had stabilized. It was time to move to the next goal.

Cheerio stood up abruptly and headed into the house. Mindy begged, "Don't run away. I'm too tired to chase you tonight. Can't we have a calm talk like two reasonable adults?"

"I'm not running," Cheerio said, resignation tingeing her voice. "I need a beer if I'm going to listen to this scheme without turning into a babbling lunatic." She went into the house. She was back in a second carrying a beer. She eased down on a chaise with a guarded look on her face and said, "Lay it on me. You want to adopt a kid?" She looked hopeful. "Couldn't we get a cat instead? Even fifteen cats?"

"No adoption," Mindy said. "I want the pregnancy almost as much as I want the baby. I'm saying I want to *have* a baby."

Cheerio tumbled off the chaise and onto the grass. She kicked her feet and pounded her fists against the ground and groaned, "Take me, God. End it right here and now. Please. I'm begging."

"I've already talked to a lawyer," Mindy continued, overlooking Cheerio's hopefully temporary insanity. "Her name's Shandra. I found her in the phone book. She said I could file a sex discrimination suit against the school board if they try to dismiss me for being single and pregnant."

"It seems like you're leaving out a big part of all this," Cheerio said, looking up at Mindy with pleading eyes.

"I called Daddy this afternoon." Mindy twisted on a strand of hair. "We had a screaming fight. He refused to loan us money for an artificial insemination, for moral reasons, you know. He also said since he co-signed the bank note with us, he'll stop us if we try to take out a second mortgage on the house to pay for things. Would your parents help if we asked?"

"They're struggling since Dad had his heart surgery."

"That's what I thought," Mindy said, sighing. "Given our present income, expected raises, rate of inflation and so forth, I estimate it will take us roughly five years, seven months, and twenty-two days to save enough nickels and dimes for the procedure. I don't want to wait that long."

"Why are you always so god-damn precise?" Cheerio sounded like she was gritting her teeth.

"I'm a mathematician."

Cheerio pitched her beer can onto the patio. She lit a cigarette and studied her tennis shoes. Her head was wreathed in smoke. Mindy said, "I've assembled three men to pick from. They're all excellent physical specimens. I can't say I particularly like any of them, but that's not important. I can tolerate them for as long as need be."

"How can you 'assemble' men?"

Mindy tucked her chin behind a shoulder, pouted her lips and batted her lashes. Cheerio rubbed her eyes, puffed out a ton of smoke and said, "I get the point. But this is god-damn goofy, Melinda. Please, please listen to me. Dykes *can't* do this. Dykes *don't* do this."

"Really," Mindy said. "I suppose I missed that section when I read The Lesbian's Hand Manual."

"What I'm saying," Cheerio said, rubbing a cheek, trying to be patient, her eyebrows knitted together, "is you're in bad shape if you think you can be a dyke and still have a life with a picture of the wife and kids on your key chain and all that shit like straights do."

"I have a different opinion."

Cheerio cleared her throat. "Do you know what you're asking of me?"

"Do you know what I'm asking of myself?"

Cheerio walked to the pile of smoldering leaves, gave it a good kick and walked to the back of the yard. She stood there so long it finally got dark enough she all but disappeared. Mindy finally saw her walking back. She gave the pile of leaves another good kick. "Are you trying to go straight on me?" Cheerio asked, sounding afraid and teary. Her tennis shoe was smoking. "Have you gotten your house and now you want to throw me out in the cold and move some guy in? If that's true, go ahead and tell me."

"I'm not saying I'm unhappy with our life," Mindy said gently, hating the fear and tears in Cheerio's voice. "I'm saying I want to have a baby. It's important to me as a woman." She paused. "Do you want to have the baby instead of me?"

"I've never even dated a guy," Cheerio said. "I'm not about to start fucking one at this late date."

"I will. For a baby."

Cheerio flipped her cigarette into the pile of leaves. "We can talk about this later." She went into the house.

Mindy followed. "When will later get here?" she asked. Cheerio didn't answer. They wandered through the house, Mindy asking, Cheerio ignoring, until Cheerio finally wandered into the great room and sat on the couch. Mindy said, "When I make up my mind about something, I'm ready to go ahead and do it."

"You're headstrong." Cheerio frowned at the ceiling. "I need to paint the ceiling in here one of these days. I've got a gallon of paint left in the garage from when we moved in. That should be enough."

"I've tried to put worms on a fishhook that didn't squirm as much as you."

" We *could* give a baby a good home," Cheerio said grudgingly, swiping at a tear that leaked out of her eye. "Can't you see the position I'm in? If I say no I might lose you, and if I say yes I might lose you. I want you to be happy so go ahead and do whatever makes you happy. But I don't want to hear any of the details. Just don't bring any guys into the house. I couldn't handle that." She walked out. Mindy heard her banging around in the garage a few minutes later.

Mindy went to her. The first thing she noticed when she got to the garage was Vincent Van Cheerio standing there with an absent-minded expression on her face. She was holding a paintbrush and a drop cloth. "So, is everything settled?" Mindy asked.

"Have you seen my putty knife?" Cheerio replied. "There's a hole in the garage wall I need to patch. It looks like some horse's ass stabbed a screwdriver into the wall. I don't know who did it, but someone around here did."

*****

Johnny Sanridge was a sportswriter for the local newspaper. Mindy had met him at her school when he was covering a basketball game during the state play-offs. He was thirty years old, with black hair and brown eyes. He was exactly her height, which meant she didn't feel gawky around him.

Their first date was five days after Mindy discussed her baby plans with Cheerio. Johnny took her to a minor league baseball game. It was part-work and part-date since he had to write a story about the game. After the game they went for a drink and chatted about things like basketball and how she liked living in Oklahoma and what Kentucky was like. Johnny told her about the two little girls he was raising by himself because his wife had died of leukemia. One of his daughters was five and one was three.

For their second date, Mindy drove to Johnny's house to meet his daughters. She immediately fell in love with them. They were the sweetest things. She got to help them take a bath and put on their pajamas. After the bath, she got on the couch with them, one on each side of her, and read Dr. Seuss to them before they went to bed. It was fun. She could tell the girls loved it, too. Especially when she put in all the 'goshes!' and 'oh, mys!' and 'wows!' that kids loved. It reminded her of when her sisters had been little and she'd read Dr. Seuss to them.

Johnny watched her with a wistful expression on his face while she read to the girls. Mindy knew what he was thinking. If any man in the world was absolutely hunting for a wife and mother, it was Johnny Sanridge. He was stalking her as much as she was stalking him.

After the girls were all tucked in and snoozing away, Johnny and Mindy went back to the living room and sat on the couch.

You Light The Fire

"You're fantastic with Heather and Marcie," Johnny said. "I can tell they think a lot of you even after only a few hours."

"They're darlings," Mindy said, thinking: *I wish they were mine.*

"They're growing up with an important piece missing from their lives since Marsha died," Johnny remarked.

"I can imagine." Mindy sipped her diet Coke, studying Johnny's face. He had a hungry look in his eyes.

"You're a lot of woman, Mindy," Johnny said. "The only woman I've brought home since Marsha died."

"I'm flattered."

"My daughters mean everything to me," Johnny sighed. "I'm not looking to get involved in a relationship that's not leading somewhere. Leading to a commitment. It wouldn't be fair to the woman or to me or to my daughters most importantly."

"I understand," Mindy said, making her decision. "I better go home now."

"Can I call you again?"

"I can't think of a reason why you should," Mindy said. "If we get involved I can guarantee you'll get hurt and I don't want to do that. You've been hurt enough, too."

"I see." Johnny smiled. A tired-looking smile. "Wrapped up in your career and not looking for a ready-made family. I've heard that story before."

"Something like that," Mindy said.

When she got home, Cheerio was in the backyard. Actually, she was perched on the roof beside the chimney. Holding a flashlight in one hand and shining it on the roof, she was pounding on something with the hammer in her other hand. Mindy stepped out on the patio and said, "Don't you want to know how my evening went?"

A diet Coke can dropped from the sky and clunked onto the cement beside Mindy. Diet Coke and foam spewed everywhere and soaked her dress. She jumped back and swiped at her dress and yelled something unladylike.

Cheerio hung her face over the gutter. "Did that almost hit you?" she asked, with all the innocence of Judas. "I'm sorry. I must've kicked it by accident."

"I'm going to change and have a late-night snack," Mindy said. "Want anything?"

"I had a cold Spam sandwich a while ago. Didn't you eat dinner?"

"I fixed dinner for Johnny and his daughters," Mindy said. "We had ribeye steaks and French fries. And salad with Ranch dressing. And garlic toast. That was hours ago, though."

Cheerio's hammer dropped from the sky and clunked onto the cement at Mindy's feet. Mindy beat a more or less hasty retreat into the house.

"Mindy?" Cheerio's voice came echoing down the chimney.

Mindy walked over to the hearth and sat down. "I'm here, darling," she yelled in her sweetest voice.

"How long will you have to fuck this guy?" Cheerio asked. "I mean, can't it be just one time? Can't you arrange it during your fertile time?"

"I will," Mindy said softly. "But even if I get pregnant the first time, I won't know it for a while, weeks, I suppose. I can't do it once and then stop to wait and see and then do it again. Once a man starts sleeping with a woman he wants her every time they're together, I think. I'll have to keep doing it until I know for sure I'm pregnant."

"And you'll be sleeping at his place once you start? And cooking him breakfast in the morning? And running around in one of his shirts after he fucks you?"

"I suppose. That's how things work, isn't it?"

Cheerio wailed, long and drawn out and plaintive, her voice echoing inside the chimney. "Cheerio, baby," Mindy pleaded, "come inside and let me fix you something to eat and rub your back. All you have to do is hang with me. It will be over soon and we'll have a baby and everything will be perfect. Just remember, being with whatever man I pick won't mean anything to me. I'll close my eyes and think of you every time."

"I'm not coming down," Cheerio wailed. "Go to bed and leave me alone. I want to be alone."

*****

Kyle Wentworth was a loan officer at the bank where Cheerio and Mindy got their house loan. He had brown hair, puppyish brown eyes and a brown beard. He had a voice like a radio announcer. When Mindy called him he sounded like he was about to drop his teeth. "I've never had a girl call me for a date," he blurted. "Where would you like to go? Would you like to fly to Bermuda for the weekend?"

Mindy almost dropped her own teeth. She started to slam the phone down because that was the rudest suggestion she'd heard in quite some time. But Kyle quickly inserted, "I'm not suggesting anything inappropriate. We would have separate hotel rooms." Mindy made her own suggestion that they go some place simple since it was a first date. They agreed on dinner at Tubby's.

Tubby's was an out-of-the-way hamburger joint with dim lights and candles on the tables and a kitchen you could see from the dining room. Mindy had a cheeseburger, fries and a diet Coke. For once, she didn't accidentally squeeze her meat into her lap and she felt grateful to whoever was in charge of such things. She'd done that one time in a restaurant and it had been practically the most embarrassing moment of her life. She doubted it was the type of behavior that would impress a prospective father.

Kyle walked her to the door when he took her home. After several minutes of throat clearing, foot shuffling, and talking about the weather, he tried to kiss her. Mindy offered a cheek. "Can I see you again?" Kyle asked.

"Give me a few days to chew on it," Mindy replied. "You're definitely in the running."

"Running for what?" Kyle looked puzzled. He stroked his beard.

"You'll find out, if and when the time comes." Mindy went into the house. Cheerio was asleep at the dining room table with a pencil clutched in her left hand. She was a southpaw, which explained most of her goofiness. A half-eaten bologna sandwich and a piece of paper with musical notes printed on it was in front of her. Written across the top of the paper was, 'God, If You're A Guy, I Hate Your Guts.'

"Let's go to bed," Mindy said, shaking Cheerio's shoulder. Cheerio jerked awake, swiped at her mouth and stumbled into the bedroom. She flopped down on the bed without even undressing. "Cock-sucker," she murmured before she went back to sleep.

"I guess that's an accurate description of me," Mindy said softly. "But it's not one I like."

*****

Mindy met Tim Merick one afternoon on the way home from school. She noticed him loafing beside the street on his motorcycle, halfheartedly pointing his radar gun at cars. On impulse, she stomped on the gas pedal and streaked by him going maybe sixty miles per hour. Tim came flying after her with his little red light flashing and his siren going, 'wheeeee.' She pulled into the parking lot of a shopping center.

Tim parked behind her, got slowly off his motorcycle and swaggered up to her window. He propped a foot on her front tire, hooked his thumbs in his gun belt and said, "Where's the fire, lady?" He chuckled at his own satirical joke.

"You're sure being nonchalant," Mindy said. "What if I was a dangerous criminal with a gun?"

Tim glanced through her windshield. "I've never seen a dangerous criminal with legs like that," he said.

Mindy tugged at her hem. "Am I going to get a ticket?" she whined with a huge smile. "I can't really afford one."

Tim laughed. "We both know you're not getting ticketed. Don't we?"

*****

The next day they had their first date. Mindy noted that Tim was an inch or two taller than her and had brown hair, brown eyes, a strong nose and a neatly-trimmed moustache. His skin was the same rich shade of black as a chocolate bar. Five seconds after Tim picked her up, Mindy decided he belonged in a nut house, mostly because he drove practically a zillion miles per hour, shifting gears like a race driver, and weaving in and out of traffic. He played soul music at brain-jarring volume on his stereo, too.

"Aren't you afraid of getting a ticket?" she shouted, clutching the seat with both her hands.

"Cops don't write other cops speeding tickets!" Tim shouted back. "Professional courtesy!"

They went to a modest brick house about three miles from Mindy's school. One of the married officers on Tim's shift lived there. There were twenty people, all young policemen and their wives or girlfriends, mingling in the backyard. Eight toddlers were splashing in a plastic pool under a tree in the back part of the yard. All the men wore shorts and half-unbuttoned shirts. The women were wearing bright blouses and shorts or filmy, summery dresses.

Mindy couldn't help noticing Tim was the only black person there. She also couldn't help noticing all the men had bulges on their hips beneath their shirts, Tim included. She decided if nothing else, she was standing in the safest spot in the world. There were probably enough guns within thirty feet of her to outshoot an entire army.

Tim took her around and introduced her to everyone. The only introduction she remembered was a woman named Lois with red hair who said, "So you're Tim's latest. He runs through girls like most men run through beer. Looks like he went for a gorgeous vacuum-head this time."

Mindy certainly thought that was a pretty rude thing to say, but she didn't start a fight. Besides, she knew for a fact she wasn't a vacuum-head. Not all the time, anyway.

She spent five minutes chatting with the toddlers when she reached the pool. They seemed thrilled to have an adult in their world, especially since she was an expert on the intricacies of splashing in a plastic pool by the time their conversation ended.

"So I'm your latest?" Mindy asked Tim after the introductions finished. They were standing with six other people on the patio, pretending they weren't choking on the charcoal smoke that blew in their faces occasionally. Mindy was sipping her usual diet Coke. Everyone else was swilling beer.

Tim laughed. "Isn't that everyone's goal in life? To make everyone else jealous?"

Mindy felt more or less confused. Why would she feel jealous over Tim? She'd hate to see a tree fall on his head, but she was otherwise indifferent about what happened to him so long as it didn't affect her.

"Do you think I'm a vacuum-head?" she asked.

"I don't like vacuum-heads," Tim replied.

"I don't like mirrored sunglasses," Mindy said. "I don't like looking at someone and seeing myself. It's too surrealistic for my taste."

Tim smiled at her and took off his sunglasses. "I was only teasing," Mindy said.

"No kidding," Tim said, but he left his sunglasses off.

Mindy had a hot dog with mustard, sweet relish and ketchup. She also had five Ruffles potato chips. While she ate, she sat in a lawn chair beside a blond woman with great legs who was a salesperson for a radio station. The woman talked about what a stressful life it was being married to a cop—how she paced a trench in the carpet if her husband was even five minutes late getting home, how she always worried if he'd been shot in a vital organ and was dead or only on the way to the hospital with a serious injury.

Mindy listened without commenting except for the occasional, obligatory, "Oh, you poor thing!" or "How awful!" She thought it was a rude dinner subject. Especially when she was eating something that could pass for one of a man's vital organs.

On the way home, Mindy said, "Have you ever shot anyone with that thing?" pointing at the bulge on Tim's hip. "Have you ever killed anyone?"

"I shot a burglar two years ago," Tim said. "He lived. Why?"

"When we first met I thought you had the capacity to be a killer. Your eyes reminded me of pictures of sharks I've seen."

Tim gave her one of the expressionless looks he was good at giving. Mindy felt so...controlled riding in a car with him. He was a powerful person. She couldn't imagine him getting into any situation he couldn't control. She could picture him riding a horse and roping cattle and slaughtering Native Americans and buffaloes.

When they got home, Tim put an arm around her waist and walked her to the door. She decided she didn't like the way his gun felt when it poked through his shirt and into her side. She didn't like guns. She wasn't certain she wanted guns in her life for any reason. She certainly didn't want guns in her baby's life or Cheerio's life, either.

"Can I come in?" Tim asked after they got to the door. He tried to kiss her. Mindy offered her cheek and replied, "No, thank you."

"Can I see you again?"

"Give me a few days to chew on it. You're definitely in the running," Mindy replied because Tim was an excellent physical specimen, and she didn't care if her baby was biracial so long as she got a baby.

"Running for what?" Tim looked as puzzled as Kyle had when told the same thing.

"You'll find out if and when the time comes." Mindy went inside. The first thing she did was stomp through the house looking for Cheerio. She found the blond witch sunbathing on a chaise in the backyard in a white string bikini that was more or less dazzling.

Alysa was sunbathing on a chaise, too, in a light green bikini that was filled to overflowing in all the right places. Alysa's chaise was sitting maybe two millimeters from Cheerio's. Mindy felt a strong urge to kill because of the way Alysa was smiling seductively and fondling Cheerio's shoulder while they chatted.

On the other side of the patio, Sherry was sitting at the picnic table, seasoning hamburger patties in-between shooing flies off the plate of pickles and tomatoes and onions. Jo was slapping the patties on the smoker as they were seasoned and helping shoo flies. Both were wearing floppy straw hats.

The backyard looked totally inviting. Music was playing, everyone was drinking beer and talking and laughing and practically having a high old time, while Mindy had burned her Sunday afternoon on a bunch of John Waynes who thought shooting people full of holes and electrocuting the ones who lived were fun activities.

It was god-damn irritating.

Stepping out onto the patio, Mindy hissed, "Cheerio Monroe, I'm ready to take your scrawny throat in my hands and squeeze until your head pops off!" She squeezed her hands together to demonstrate. "I happened to look in the garage when I came home. My Mustang is covered in leaves and mud and sticks. What happened?"

Cheerio pretended to be puzzled. She poked a hand inside her bikini and scratched a breast. Finally she said, "I had to rake out the flower beds a while back. I was flinging leaves and shit everywhere. Maybe the wind blew some of it on your car."

"Hah!" Mindy snapped. "My car's been sitting in the garage all day. How could the wind blow mud all the way from the front of the house to the garage and onto my car when your Spitfire, which just happens to be sitting in the garage beside my Mustang, is spotless? Answer me that if you can."

Cheerio shrugged. "Ain't life strange," she sneered. Alysa snorted. Mindy said, "Don't you want to know how my afternoon went?"

Cheerio put on her toothy 'bite my bottom' smile. "I don't think much of the po-lice," she said. "I guess I don't have the proper respect for authority symbols."

Alysa held her nose. "Pee-yew," she drawled. "You need to shower, sugar puss. You smell like you've been rolling with pigs."

"Want a burger, doll?" Sherry asked. "I'll pat you out a big fat one." She squinted out from under the brim of her hat. Her eyes looked as mournful as a basset hound's.

"I can't!" Mindy bellowed. "I have to wash my car. I can't drive to school tomorrow in a trash-mobile. What would everyone think of me?"

Cheerio practically chortled. Mindy said, "If you four will pitch in and help, we can wash my car in no time. Then I can join you. It's not too late to salvage part of my weekend."

Everyone studied their hands. Mindy finally said, "Cheerio, why are you acting this way? I thought I was doing this with your approval."

"We'll keep our problems to ourselves," Cheerio snapped. She looked nail-biting angry.

"Can we talk later?"

Cheerio squirted suntan lotion on her stomach. Alysa sat up and went to rubbing the lotion all over Cheerio's stomach. Cheerio fondled Alysa's shoulder during the rubbing.

Mindy felt an urge to grind her teeth down to stubs. She stomped into the house, hid behind the door and eavesdropped. Not that she cared what everyone was saying about her. Not much, anyway. Cheerio and Alysa started talking about a restaurant in New York City they'd both been to. Sherry and Jo talked about how bad the flies were this year. Everyone acted like she didn't even exist, like she was dead. It stung more than if they'd said every hateful thing in the world about her. She couldn't believe she felt unwelcome in her own home.

When Tim called two days later, Mindy said, "I don't want to see you again. Your swaggering machismo gives me a headache. I don't like guns, anyway."

"That's fine with me," Tim replied, sounding murderous. "A vice cop from the cook-out pulled me aside this morning. She said she's seen you before, at The Eager Beaver on Seventy-ninth Street. That's a hard-core dyke bar. Everyone was laughing at me and I didn't know it."

Mindy couldn't say she particularly liked herself right then. Not when she was marching roughshod over everyone around her and causing them, and herself, unhappiness—all over a need she had, a need other people might say was foolish, but a need that was inside of her just the same and wasn't something she could deny. She decided to just close her mind to everything and everybody around her. She couldn't let anything distract her because there was no way she was turning back. Not when she'd come so far.

CHAPTER 7

Seven o'clock Friday morning. She was excited over an upcoming day teaching derivatives, and hopeful that she could leave early enough to stop at Quick Trip for a jelly doughnut and a small plastic bottle of orange juice. When her train of thought was interrupted by the phone ringing, Mindy was practically furious. Who would be stupid enough to call at seven in the morning when she was rushing around trying to get ready for school? She ran into the bedroom. Cheerio was perched on the edge of the bed, holding her head in her hands and groaning, "Oh, God. Oh, God," over and over. Cheerio was not exactly what you'd call a morning person.

Mindy snatched up the phone. "Hello?"

"Have you had time to chew on things?" Kyle asked.

"I've decided I'll see you again." Mindy sat on the bed and tried tugging her hose on with one hand. She bit her lip to keep from grunting into the phone. That would certainly have been unladylike.

"Great!" Kyle declared. "I was hoping you would."

"Hang on a sec." Mindy tossed the phone on the bed, tugged on her hose and slithered into her dress. She picked up the phone as she sat back down to put on her heels. "Hello? Are you there?"

"I got to the office early and thought I'd give you a call," Kyle said. "I can't think of a better way to start a day than hearing your sweet voice."

"Oh." Mindy studied her reflection in the mirror. Her hair was giving her fits. Maybe she should shave her head bald. "Where did you want to take me?"

"Would you like going to Arlington to see Six Flags and a famous wax museum tomorrow?" Kyle asked.

"Where is Arlington? I thought Six Flags was in Atlanta. I'm not going to Atlanta on a date with you or anyone else."

Kyle laughed his methodical radio announcer's laugh. "Arlington is in-between Dallas and Fort Worth. There's a Six Flags there, too."

"Texas seems an awfully long way to go on a date," Mindy mused aloud. "I don't like roller coasters, anyway. I'm always afraid of tumbling out and mashing my face on the ground." Was she being trés-trés-cute or what?

"I promise to pick you up at eight in the morning and have you home by midnight," Kyle said, sounding like a patient father-figure. "You don't have to ride a roller coaster."

"I've never been to Texas but I'm not sure I think much of going there," Mindy said. "My roommate Cheerio, you remember her, I'm sure. My cousin Cheerio? She's lived in Tulsa for years and she doesn't speak very highly of Texas. She claims anyone who lives in Oklahoma should hate Texas."

"Texas is okay," Kyle said.

"I have to be home by midnight for sure or I turn into a troll." More trés-trés-cuteness. "See you in the morning. 'Bye." Mindy slammed the phone down. "Do you need CPR?" she asked Cheerio. "You're going to be late for work."

"Caffeine," Cheerio mumbled, giving her crotch a good scratch. "Nicotine. Anything that ends in i-n-e."

"Cheerio, I'm dying," Mindy groveled. "Do we have time for a quickie? I'll make the time if you will."

"And give up my coffee?" Cheerio grunted. She staggered out of the bedroom and headed toward the kitchen.

Mindy rushed back to the bathroom to finish getting ready. What with Kyle calling and then getting rebuffed by Cheerio and then messing with her hair and then poking eyeliner in her left eye, she was almost tardy for school, and no, she didn't get a jelly doughnut. She wondered if her principal would have made her stay for detention if she had been tardy. He made the kids stay for detention when they were tardy.

*****

"It's driving me stark-raving-bonkers," Cheerio said, picking up her tray and moving to a table with Bonnie and Sue and Sally. The cafeteria was filled with chattering refinery workers, wolfing down shitty cafeteria food on their lunch break. "A baby. I still can't believe it."

Bonnie and Sue and Sally clicked their tongues and looked sympathetic. They were all three straight married girls, but Cheerio didn't hold that against them. They always got together at lunch and bitched about their mates. Bonnie and Sue and Sally would complain about their husbands, saying, "That worthless, lazy bastard comes home every night and throws his socks right in the middle of my clean floor."

Cheerio would say, "Hhmmm," and think about how Mindy always said the same thing about Cheerio's hose. Bonnie and Sue and Ann would whine, "He never helps with any of the cooking or cleaning or shopping. All he does is come home and eat dinner and drink a beer and fart a few times and go to bed."

Hhmmm again.

Cheerio took a bite of her tuna fish sandwich. It tasted like shit, but then everything she ate lately tasted like shit. Stress. She'd lost five pounds in the last three weeks, and her brush was full of hair after every time she used it, and her period was coming and going, spotting, like it had never heard of a monthly schedule. If Mindy didn't get knocked up pretty soon Cheerio Monroe would be a walking skeleton—if she didn't drop dead from a massive heart attack before then.

"I don't mean to be insensitive," Bonnie said, peering over her glasses, crunching on a potato chip. "But this whole thing makes my mind reel. The thought of one woman being jealous because another woman is seeing men, why, it causes me to pause and consider the entire meaning of the universe or something."

"Well," Cheerio said, forcing down a swallow of tuna. "It's kinda like this. If she was seeing another woman, I could handle it better. I'd try harder to be all she needs in a woman. But how can I be more of a guy than any guy she's seeing? How would you feel if your husbands started dating another guy?"

Bonnie shaped her hand like a pistol and acted like she was blowing her brains out. "Don't you like kids?" Sue asked.

"Sure," Cheerio said. "I love kids, and I'd love having one. It's the way we have to do it that bugs me."

"You're not afraid of losing Mindy, are you?" Bonnie asked. "Isn't she just as much a lesbo as you are? I mean, you've been together what, over four years? And you had that marriage-commitment thingy we all went to last year."

Cheerio stood up, carried her tray to the waste basket and went back to work, even though she had another fifteen minutes of lunch break. She started working her way through an invoice for thirty weight oil that had come in that morning, but her mind wasn't on what she was doing. Her mind was on Mindy.

Oh, sure enough, Mindy said all the right things, she was reassuring and comforting. But the doubts, the god-damn doubts, were always there, always in the back of Cheerio's mind. She didn't know guys, didn't know what they said to women they wanted to fuck, didn't know if a guy could say something to a woman that would make her ignore the fact that she was a dyke and make her want to be what America wanted her to be—especially when the dyke had a tender personality like Mindy and was eager to please like Mindy.

It was the not knowing that was the worst. If the getting pregnant had involved Mindy seeing another woman, Cheerio would've been jealous, sure enough, but she could've handled it.

You Light The Fire

She could've said: *Go ahead and fuck another woman and then come back to me and I'll treat you better, I'll treat you the way you like to be treated.* But every time Mindy left home with a guy, Cheerio's stomach was in a knot the whole time, wondering if she'd get Mindy back. And when she thought of Mindy in a guy's arms, when she thought of a guy undressing Mindy and caressing her body and sticking his...she wouldn't let herself think about that.

*****

During the drive from Tulsa to Dallas Mindy finally got to see the Oklahoma everyone always wrote and sang about in songs. On and on and on the grass and cows and oil wells spread. Mindy just knew she could see for a zillion miles. It was so beautiful.

It didn't take much for her to picture lines of heartbroken Native Americans, Cherokee and Choctaw and Cheyenne, trudging across the land, herded there by soldiers like a bunch of livestock. Forced to leave their natural homes in other parts of the United States and move to Oklahoma, many had no possessions other than what they could carry on their backs. She pictured them fighting vicious battles against the Native Americans who already lived there. Struggling to make substitute homes. Being gradually swallowed up, until they, and eventually even their society, ceased to exist for all practical purposes.

In her mind's eye she also saw covered wagons filled with women and children, fathers carrying guns to protect their families from wild animals and outlaws. Also to kill food so their families wouldn't starve to death before the wild animals and outlaws could kill them. Mothers wearing bonnets and nursing babies. Older children staring wide-eyed at their new surroundings. Thousands of families searching for new homes during one of the great land rushes. Just as she had come to Oklahoma in search of a new home, except instead of riding in a covered wagon, she was looking at the same land for the first time through the tinted window of a red Mercedes with tan leather interior.

She felt so much sadness and so many dashed hopes and forgotten dreams and screams of despair all around her. All combined together to become this land that held so many memories of the past and so much promise for the future all at the same time. Mindy became a true Okie on that bright Saturday morning. She felt so proud of her adopted state. Such a tragic, colorful, romantic history.

South of McAlester, Oklahoma, she saw her first ever armadillo. It was mashed flat in the middle of the road, and she felt cheated. "Have you ever seen an armadillo?" she asked Kyle.

He nodded. "Dozens."

"What do armadillos normally do?"

Kyle looked thoughtful. "I can't say," he said. "The ones I've seen have been pancakes in the road."

"Isn't there a song about getting drunk with armadillos?" Mindy asked, bobbing her head for emphasis, feeling like she was about to puke from her own cuteness. "I'm sure I heard it one time. Maybe that's why armadillos are mashed on the road. They're always getting drunk and staggering in front of cars."

Kyle looked at her like she had three 36D's. Mindy heaved a sigh. Maybe she could get a laugh if she told him the one about the traveling lesbian salesperson, the elephant, the banana and the boiled egg. She poked Kyle in the ribs and said, "Hello? Are you alive? Is there a person inside that body?" She all of a sudden missed Cheerio so badly it almost hurt physically. She spent the rest of the drive thinking about Cheerio and wondering what fun things she had planned for the day. Cheerio had been asleep when Mindy left home.

The wax museum was fun. There was a section with Dracula and Frankenstein and all sorts of other scary statues. Every once in a while a red light would flash on and a scary statue would appear. Mindy squealed obligingly when they went through and let Kyle put his arm around her. She wasn't really scared, though. It was just a bunch of wax dummies, after all. And even if Dracula or Frankenstein had come to life and jumped out at her, she would have reared back and booted him in the nuts and that would've been that.

They decided not to brave the enormous crowd at Six Flags. Kyle took her to downtown Dallas instead. They drove along the route President Kennedy's motorcade had taken the day he was assassinated. Downtown was practically deserted so Kyle parked. They walked half a block and sat on a bench across from the building where the shots had been fired. Mindy knew it was a special place. But it didn't feel like a special place. It was just a downtown. Tall buildings. An occasional car passed, and every so often she saw people walking on the sidewalks. It was warm and sunny. A breeze ruffled her hair. It was Downtown Anywhere on a Saturday afternoon, and...yet...it wasn't. How could a place be so special and feel so un-special all at the same time?

Mindy remembered the day President Kennedy died. She had run home from school that day and burst into the house, screeching the news like no one knew it except her. Mother had slapped her face and said, "Shut up your screeching in the house. You were raised better than that." Then Mother had said, "Everyone knew it was only a matter of time until they got that rich Catholic boy." Mother's actions confused the dickens out of Mindy, and it wasn't until years later that she decided Mother wasn't uncaring, but was merely a Republican Baptist instead.

When they got home, Kyle asked, "Can I see you again?"

"Yes. You're definitely the Number One Contender."

"You have to be the most mysterious girl I've ever known," Kyle said. He grabbed her arms and pulled her close, close enough she could feel his breath on her eyelashes. "I don't know whether to be enchanted by you or disgusted with you," he whispered.

Mindy pooh-poohed him. Kyle tried to kiss her. She offered a cheek, pulled away and went into the house. There was a note from Cheerio on the coffee table. The note said, 'Went out to get drunk. No big deal. I like being alone on Saturday night.'

Mindy waited long enough for Kyle to have gotten home before she called him. He sounded pleased. Mindy said, "I want to meet your family. Parents, grandparents. The works."

"Great," Kyle said enthusiastically. "I'll arrange everything for next Saturday night."

"How about Friday night?" Mindy suggested, remembering Cheerio's note. "I'm busy on Saturday."

"Okay." Kyle hesitated before softly saying, "Mindy, I had a great time today. I think I'm in love with you."

"Don't say that!" Mindy blurted, feeling shocked. "Good night."

Cheerio, Alysa and the other four women in Silky Wet came boiling into the house at three in the morning. Everyone was more or less bombed. They attacked the kitchen like a swarm of locusts. In no time flat they managed to pull out every pot and pan in the house, even though none of them knew what to do with the pots and pans once they were pulled out, and piled cheese and bacon and eggs all over the counter. Mindy stood in the door in her robe with what she knew was a murderous expression.

"Look at her face," Cheerio sneered. "She's worried about money. That's all she cares about lately."

Alysa bragged, "The great and famous Alysa Leigh pays her own way." She took a hundred dollar bill from a pocket and walked over to Mindy. Mindy said, "I don't want that." Alysa slipped her hand inside Mindy's robe and poked the money into Mindy's panties. Alysa left her hand there for a second, looking at Mindy with a mocking expression. Her eyes were glassy, she smelled like beer.

"Move it or lose it, Mary," Mindy snapped. Alysa traced a fingernail up between Mindy's breasts and tickled her chin before swaggering back to the stove where she was burning scrambled eggs. Mindy pulled the money out of her panties and tossed it on the floor.

"This was the greatest night of my life!" Cheerio said. She giggled and stuffed a piece of cheddar cheese into her mouth. The other women cracked up.

"What happened?" Mindy asked.

"She got up and sang with us," Alysa said. "Or tried to. She sucked." Alysa snorted. "Look at her. She was stumbling around the stage, slurring her words, missing her breaks, forgetting lyrics. They booed her off the stage." She pounded a wooden spoon on the skillet, flashed her eyes at Cheerio and said, "You god-damn amateur! It'll be a cold day in hell before you get on a stage with me again. I don't enjoy looking like shit when I'm performing."

"Well, just go fuck yourself, Mary Smith," Cheerio said. "I've been to the top. I didn't stay there, but I've seen it. That's something you'll never see."

"You need to forget Cappie," Alysa said, her eyes flashing again, pounding the skillet again. "She was a gifted performer and a beautiful woman, but she's dead. You've got your head buried in yesterday and you're pissing all over today." She turned to Mindy and said, "Could you make us some biscuits? None of us can make biscuits except out of a can and you don't keep any around here. Your kitchen is like something out of the eighteen hundreds."

"Cheerio, come to bed," Mindy said softly. "You don't need to be letting these people make a fool out of you."

"No!" Cheerio snapped, putting on her stubborn look. Mindy cooked breakfast for everyone since it was the only way she could spend time with Cheerio.

*****

That Friday, Mindy showered as soon as she got home from school to get the smell of chalk dust off. She also shaved. She certainly didn't want to be a hairy ape when she met Kyle's family, or rather, scrutinized Kyle's family. She decided to wear a streamlined black dress with a front slit, an elasticized back bodice and spaghetti straps, which she halter-tied. The hem was set five inches above the knee. Black hose completed the outfit, except for shoes.

She pulled out her inch-and-a-half black heels, put them on, took them off, put on black Loafers, looked in the mirror and hated the way the Loafers ruined the impact of her dress. Kyle claimed he was five-ten, but Mindy knew he was only bragging. She decided not to worry about towering over Kyle and put her inch-and-a-half heels back on because Kyle's family already knew he was short.

Cheerio got home as she had her foot lifted to her bottom to dab some perfume on her ankle. Cheerio sucked in her breath and moaned, "What a sexy pose. You're stunning."

"Thanks."

"It's not for me, is it?"

"Not this time," Mindy said. She checked her lipstick. "I'm working tonight."

"You mean you're fucking him tonight," Cheerio said flatly. She walked out. A few seconds later Mindy heard her car squeal out of the driveway.

Kyle's parents lived on the south side. Mindy was impressed. She'd lived in Tulsa long enough to know the south side was the ritziest part of town. The house was on the edge of a golf course, on top of a hill, and was three stories high. The white stucco and tall white columns on the front gleamed in the sunlight. There were two BMWs, one Jaguar, three Porsches, two Cadillacs and one white Rolls-Royce parked in the circular drive. Mindy had seen more insecurity-inspiring houses. In pictures.

A grey-haired butler with a British accent and wearing a black uniform met them at the door. An elegant-looking woman in her mid-forties with long brown hair, green eyes and wearing a white evening gown was right behind the butler.

Kyle's mother.

Mrs. Wentworth shook Mindy's hand and said, "It's lovely to meet you, Miss Brinson. Kyle has told us a great deal about you." She took Mindy's elbow and steered her toward a room on the left of the entrance hall, just in front of the winding staircase. She cooed, "You're the first girl Kyle has chosen to introduce us to in years and years, since college, I believe. We were beginning to think he's a dedicated bachelor."

"I'm flattered," Mindy offered.

"Oh, your voice." Mrs. Wentworth stopped dead in her tracks.

"I beg your pardon?"

" 'Ah beg yuh pahduhn?' " Mrs. Wentworth mimicked, pretending to be confused. She snickered. "Have you considered speech therapy for your accent?" She pretended to be dismayed. "Don't take me wrong. I'm not saying I dislike it. I think Southern accents are amusingly quaint. But some people think they're so unpolished." She started walking again.

Mindy didn't say anything. She was too busy biting her tongue and doing a not-so-slow burn to talk.

The room they walked into was plush, to say the least. Heavy-looking, overstuffed furniture, an abundance of marble and crystal knickknacks, dead animal heads on one of the walls, a huge stone fireplace in one corner. There were eight or ten zillion people perched on the furniture, sipping from sparkling crystal wine glasses.

Mrs. Wentworth gaily called, "Cindy's here everybody!" All the people stood and galloped toward Mindy like a herd of starving hogs to a single ear of corn, causing her bottom to practically pucker and making her wonder just who the hell was scrutinizing whom.

"Mother, you do have a flair for the dramatic," Kyle chastised, using the same tone of voice Mindy used on her students when they misbehaved. "But her name is Mindy," he added. "And couldn't you have introduced her less dramatically?"

Mrs. Wentworth pressed a hand to her throat. "Oh, my," she remarked, eyes widening. "Do social situations frighten you, my dear?"

"No," Mindy squeaked. She felt like belting the old witch. Kyle whispered soothingly, "Old money. They enjoy formality." He laughed his radio announcer's laugh and Mindy relaxed. A little.

Somehow, probably through a divine miracle, she made it through the introductions and before-dinner-cocktails-and-mingling without making a total ass of herself and dropping something in her lap. She was so thankful when the butler tinkled a little bell and they *adjourned to the dining room.* Mindy didn't know for sure, but she assumed the bell-tinkling followed by *adjourning to the dining room* meant it was time for face-stuffing.

Naturally, being a small-town clod and all, she almost dropped her teeth when she walked into the dining room. She'd never seen such a grand dining room. The floor was brownish-gold parquet shiny enough to see your reflection. An enormous, round fireplace was in the middle of the dining room. The table encircled the fireplace. It was a huge wooden affair, as were the chairs. The plates looked like they were trimmed in gold. The three waiters wore outfits that looked like tuxedos.

"No paper plates and TV trays tonight, huh, Mother?" Kyle observed, shooting dear Mother a look. Mrs. Wentworth ignored him. She took Mindy's elbow and trilled, "Won't you sit between Grandmother Mitchell and me, my dear, Wendi?"

"No you don't, my dear," Kyle said. He pulled Mindy to the other side of the table and she got to sit beside Kyle's father who was much less threatening. Mr. Wentworth was an older salt-and-pepper version of Kyle, except he didn't have a beard. He did have the same puppyish brown eyes and radio announcer's voice.

Dinner started with shrimp cocktails featuring the biggest shrimp she'd ever seen. She noticed everyone else peeled their shrimp before eating them so she peeled hers, too, feeling thankful she hadn't made a nincompoop of herself by popping one in her mouth before peeling it and then having to spew shell on everyone. The main course was filet mignon wrapped in strips of bacon Mr. Wentworth said was from his cattle ranch. Mindy decided Mr. Wentworth was tolerable. He flirted with her and told bawdy jokes all during dinner. Mindy giggled self-consciously and offered the obligatory blush after each joke. Kyle watched with an amused expression on his face the whole time. His eyes said, 'You wanted it, you got it.'

When they got ready to leave, Mrs. Wentworth bussed Mindy's cheek and pronounced, "You're lovely, my dear. I'm so happy for you and Kyle. We must have lunch sometime." Mindy shot Kyle a look, wondering just exactly what he'd told dear sweet Mother dearest. He all of a sudden decided his shoes were the most interesting thing in the world.

Mrs. Wentworth touched Mindy's arm and said, "I've been wanting to ask you a question all evening, Kandi. I don't know this firsthand, but I've heard you oversized girls have difficulty buying clothes."

"That's so true," Mindy replied. "I spend a fortune on clothes at The Large and Tall Shop. Of course, I only go into the tall section. You should go there. You might find something you like in the large section." She glanced significantly at Mrs. Wentworth's hips and bottom.

Mrs. Wentworth made a choking sound.

Kyle snickered.

Walking down the sidewalk, Mindy said, "I've seen your parents' house. I'd like to see where you live now."

Kyle got her to the car and sped out of there so fast Mindy wondered if he'd maybe stuffed some of the silverware in his pockets. "Why do you work in a bank if your family is so rich?" she asked.

"I'm being groomed," Kyle said. "I don't simply work there; my family owns the bank."

Kyle's house was on a placid cul-de-sac about three miles from his parents' house. The homes, or rather mansions, in the neighborhood were spectacular, huge affairs with wood shingle roofs and porch lights that used four or five bulbs instead of just one. Kyle's house was built of brick and glass and had light brown wood trimming. A row of in-ground lights illuminated the front of the house. The lawn looked freshly mown, the shrubbery was perfectly trimmed. It looked so...staged.

"You're hateful!" Mindy exclaimed, slapping Kyle's arm. "Am I so predictable that you knew I'd want to come here tonight? You had this all planned, didn't you?"

"Uh," Kyle mumbled. Mindy slapped his arm again. He grinned, looking anything but crushed.

Inside the house, Kyle took her into the den and told her to stand in front of a sliding glass door. When she did, he flipped a switch on the wall. A zillion lights flashed on around an in-ground swimming pool. The water glistened a bright blue in the lights. Lots of padded patio furniture sat beside the pool. A stone fence surrounded the back yard.

"It's beautiful," Mindy gasped.

Kyle took a package wrapped in gold paper from his pocket. "Here," he mumbled, thrusting it into her hands.

Mindy tore off the paper. Beneath the paper was a grey felt box. Inside the box was a gold chain with a diamond pendant. Eagerly she slipped the chain around her neck. "Oh, I can't clasp it!" She stamped a foot. "My hands are shaking too much. I'm *so* excited. Will you help?" She turned her back to Kyle. She felt his moist fingers against her neck. She took a quarter-step back until she felt his crotch against her bottom. His crotch felt like you'd expect it to feel. Like a certain gerbil's name.

"Thank you, Kyle," she said, turning to face him. "I've never received such a nice gift." She fingered the diamond. "It's so delicate."

Kyle opened a smoked glass cabinet beside the fireplace. Inside was a sink and glasses and bottles of wine, even a miniature refrigerator. He poured two glasses of wine. Mindy sat on the brown velvet couch. Kyle turned on the stereo and remained standing. He stared at her crossed legs like he was hypnotized.

"Are you just going to stand there staring at me all night?" Mindy pouted her lips and looked through her lashes at him. She knew she was being a coquette but it seemed like the situation called for a certain amount of coquettishness. She drained her glass of wine and asked for a refill, hoping it would make things easier.

You Light The Fire

After Kyle filled her glass, he moved to the couch beside her. Mindy smiled at him. He kissed her, gruffly, his beard scratching her face. She opened her mouth when his tongue pressed against her lips. Kyle pushed her against the couch, one hand going under her dress to touch her, the other undoing her spaghetti straps and cupping one of her breasts. Mindy didn't fight. She didn't exactly respond, either. She just lay back on the couch, letting his clumsy hands grope her.

Kyle pulled away suddenly, his face and eyes looking excited. "You're a virgin, aren't you?" he breathed. "I thought you might be."

"No, I'm not," Mindy said, wondering if Kyle had asked the world's all-time stupidest question of a woman her age. "But there's only been one other man in my life. He was a boy, really. It was a long time ago."

Eight to the third is five hundred twelve.

Kyle looked pleased. He was probably thinking: *So you're almost a virgin.* Mindy decided not to tell him about the twenty-some-odd women she'd crawled between the sheets with in her life. "Do we need protection?" Kyle asked dutifully.

"I'm on the pill."

Eight to the fourth is four thousand ninety-six.

"Why don't you go to the bedroom and undress," Kyle coaxed, pointing down the hall. "It's the third door on the right. I'll lock up and be right there."

Clutching her bodice to her breasts, she found her way to the bedroom. She thought about Cheerio with every step and wished for another glass of wine, although she didn't know how much wine would be enough.

Eight to the fifth is thirty-two thousand seven hundred sixty-eight.

When she got to the luxurious master bedroom, the first thing she did was take off the pendant and put it on the nightstand. The second thing she did was open a window. The third thing she did was kick at the screen until it came off. The fourth thing she did was crawl out the window into the front yard and walk three blocks to the nearest Quick Trip to call a cab. She hated herself the whole time because she had aggressively pushed-pushed-pushed things until it came down to crunch time, and then she'd faltered like frightened and uncertain little girl.

She managed to keep control of herself until she paid the cab driver and started walking toward her front door. Then she all of a sudden went to braying like a hungry jackass. She wasn't going to have a baby. She wasn't strong enough to do what it took. She'd thought she was, but she wasn't. She'd never be strong enough so she'd never get to have a baby. Fine. She'd just have to accept that fact. But she was sure as the dickens going to do some squalling before she did. And she did just that as soon as she got into the house, plopping down on the couch and kicking her feet and pounding her fists and throwing what you might call a major-league petulant fit.

Just then, Cheerio came rushing through the front door, eyes red and puffy like she'd been doing her own squalling. A brown paper sack was clutched under one arm. The other arm was wrestling a wriggling ball of grey, black and white fur wearing a hot pink collar. The furball jumped out of Cheerio's arm. It was about five-inches tall and had bulging eyes and big ears. It looked like a deformed rabbit. The furball proceeded to speed around the great room, yapping its head off. Then it jumped into Mindy's lap and went, "Yap-yap-yap," and growled, sounding as vicious as a goldfish.

"Heel, you little bitch!" Cheerio bellowed about the time the furball hurled itself off Mindy's lap. It raced around the room, sniffing and inspecting everything in sight and wagging its miniature tail, and yapping some more.

"What the dickens is that creature?" Mindy wailed.

"What's wrong?" Cheerio shrieked seeing that Mindy had been crying. Her face turned as red as her eyes. "Did that chicken-shit bastard hurt you? I'll kill him!"

"I couldn't," Mindy squalled. "I just couldn't."

"There *is* a God!" Cheerio shouted gratefully. She tossed the sack on the floor. It popped open and bills flew everywhere and loose change rolled in every direction. Cheerio ran to the couch and started planting kisses all over Mindy's face. "I went begging at The Eager Beaver and every other dyke bar in town," Cheerio whispered. "Silky Wet chipped in. Sherry and Jo gave. Everybody helped. There's more than enough to pay a doctor."

"They did that for us?"

"Hey, us dykes got to stick together," Cheerio chortled, giving Mindy a hug.

The phone rang. Mindy snatched it up because she very well knew who it was. Kyle said, "What is happening? I've been tearing the house apart looking for you. I thought you were playing some kind of demure game."

Mindy promptly gave him his walking papers.

"I don't understand," Kyle said.

"It's simple. I could never love someone who leaves the toilet seat up." Mindy slammed the phone down, stretched out on the couch and did some serious caterwauling because she would get to have a baby after all. Because her friends, and even women she didn't know, wanted to help her, and not because a man wanted a piece of ass.

Cheerio flopped down on a chair with a goofy look on her face. "Mother Mary!" she blurted. "If you don't like the dog I'll take her back. It's not that big a deal. I only got her because a dyke gave me five dollars to take her. Name's Spike, by the way. That's a good name for a watchdog."

CHAPTER 8

The whole artificial insemination business was a pain in the bottom. A figurative pain in the bottom, of course. If she liked lying on a bed and spreading her legs so a man could poke a syringe of wiggly worms into her reproductive organ and then bathe her cervix for twenty minutes in the wiggly worm pool formed by the blade of a speculum, she would've let Kyle use his "speculum" on her. The way she figured things, there wasn't a great deal of difference between a leering bald-headed doctor's speculum and Kyle's "speculum." Except Kyle's would have naturally inseminated her for free, and the doctor charged an arm and a leg to do it artificially.

Not only did Dr. Slobber-and-Leer irritate her with his speculum, the counselors at the clinic irritated the dickens out of her during the sessions. One time they said, "Questions of illegitimacy frequently arise from the artificial insemination procedure since the offspring can't be registered in the father's name."

"My child isn't a piece of livestock that needs to be registered," Mindy said steadfastly. "He or she will be a Brinson, and there's nothing wrong with that."

"Ms. Brinson," the counselors persisted, "we're merely trying to counsel you on the ethical, social and legal ramifications of what you're doing. You must understand that any child resulting is at a serious potential disadvantage society-wise. You must also understand the insemination procedure is rarely conducive to the ultimate happiness of the couple involved, nor does it help the security of the relationship. The potential difficulties are increased for a lesbian couple."

Mindy blew them a raspberry. Only on the inside, though. She looked thoughtful and nodded on the outside.

Leaving the clinic, she drove to the water company, where she bought back one of her checks that had recently returned to Earth after bouncing halfway to the moon. Next, she drove to the electric company, where she bought back another check that was at T-minus-twenty-seconds-and-counting to liftoff. Buying back checks that liked pretending they were rockets was a pain in the bottom, too. Not to mention humiliating, although she was surprised her face didn't feel hot. Not too hot, anyway.

On top of everything else giving her a pain in the bottom, Alysa had recently had a virtual brawl with her latest lover and promptly got tossed out of her apartment. Cheerio just as promptly invited Alysa to move in. Mindy assumed because it was more convenient for them to stage their 'who's the biggest witch' contests if they were living under the same roof.

Three weeks after Alysa moved in, Mindy got home from a trip to Stillwater, where she'd been sent for a weekend math symposium being held at Oklahoma State University, and found Cheerio and Alysa curled up in bed together. In less than two seconds, Mindy catapulted through her stages of anger until she finally did her own blasting off for the moon. She shouted every accusation under the sun at Cheerio and Alysa. They denied everything, and claimed Alysa's water bed mattress had sprung a leak and she was sleeping in Cheerio and Mindy's bed because she didn't want to wake up drowned. They also claimed Alysa's mattress was hanging over the clothesline in the backyard with a big patch on it as proof.

"I might be stupid!" Mindy roared. "But I'm not stupid enough to believe that lame line of bull-shit!"

"Calm down and listen," Cheerio squeaked, looking half-afraid and half-mad and half-guilty. "You goofy gash-ette! I didn't know she was sleeping with me. I was alone when I came to bed. I thought she'd sleep on the couch when she got home from work."

"You're lying!" Mindy roared. "You were sure snuggled up good and tight with her when I walked in. You were practically inside her skin."

"I was asleep," Cheerio claimed. "I must've thought it was you so my instincts made me do it."

"You're still lying!" Mindy shouted. "Alysa's lover tossed her out three weeks ago so I know she's been doing without. And you, Cheerio Monroe, you little...you haven't wanted me since I started seeing the doctor, so I know you've been doing without. Or you better have been doing without. I think the two of you let your hormones get the better of you last night and attacked each other."

Alysa sat up and hissed, "I've heard enough of this! I doubt you've been catching an O from that doctor and his instruments so you're as frustrated as the rest of us. Why don't you quit bitching and climb into this bed? All three of us frustrated dykes can take care of each other."

"That's easily the most perverted thing I've heard in my life!" Mindy pronounced at just about the same time Cheerio put her feet against Alysa's back and booted her out of bed. Alysa started cussing a blue streak as soon as she hit the floor.

Mindy stomped outside to check Alysa's water bed mattress. It was hanging over the clothesline with a big patch on it, but Mindy still wasn't sure she believed a word about what had happened. She felt guilty, though, so she cooked breakfast for Cheerio and Alysa as a way of kissing ass.

After breakfast, Cheerio apologized sheepishly, "I didn't think you wanted me while you're doing this baby stuff. We can go to bed now if you want." Mindy heaved a sigh and said, "I'll take care of you, but I wouldn't enjoy it myself. Every time I spread my legs I think about Dr. Slobber-and-Leer and it ruins everything." Cheerio said she guessed she'd just keep going around frustrated until Mindy was more in the mood.

The next day, on the way home from buying back her last rubber check, Mindy stopped by Froug's Department Store to pick up a dress she'd had her eye on for some time. It was a hot pink torso-revealing two-piece with a cropped top and an elastic waist skirt with a bow, flirty peplum and back slit. It cost $44.99 plus tax, but she thought it was worth it.

Her next stop was Skaggs, where she bought two T-bones and two baking potatoes and lettuce and tomatoes and a bottle of Blue Cheese dressing and a loaf of French bread. The first thing she did after she got home and put her groceries away was grab a handful of ice cubes and march into Alysa's bedroom. Alysa was sleeping. She slept from nine or ten in the morning until seven or eight at night before she got up, put on her makeup, ate breakfast and went to wherever Silky Wet was playing.

Mindy jerked Alysa's silk sheets back and crammed the handful of ice cubes into her panties. Alysa stiffened but didn't wake up. Mindy waited patiently. All of a sudden Alysa came zipping out of bed, cussing like crazy, and proceeded to gyrate around the room doing something that closely resembled a pagan rain dance. Mindy said, "After your song and dance routine ends, get dressed and get out. I want to be alone with my lover tonight."

"Well, just go fuck yourself, Miss Knockers!" Alysa screeched, digging ice cubes out of her panties. "Can I shower first?"

"If you must."

"What time is it?"

"Four."

Alysa groaned.

Mindy went to the kitchen and broiled her steaks and baked her potatoes and fixed her salad and buttered/garlic-salted her French bread. She was just wrapping everything up to put in the oven to keep warm when Alysa walked into the kitchen.

"Are you still here?" Mindy snapped.

"Something smells good." Alysa had a wheedling look on her face. "Will you cook me breakfast before I go? Nobody, and I mean nobody, cooks like you do."

"Mary!"

"Jesus H. Christ!" Alysa flashed her eyes. "When can I come back?"

"Not before noon tomorrow."

Alysa was mumbling to herself as she left.

Mindy scampered around closing curtains and straightening the house a little. She put some elevator music on the stereo and lit four scented candles and turned back the bed and set the table. After all that, she tacked the hem on her new dress so it was exactly eight inches above the knee, more or less. The last thing she did was shower. She also shaved, not wanting to be a hairy ape when she jumped Cheerio's bones. After her shower, she freshened her makeup, put her hair in a bun and slithered into her new dress. Hot pink three-inch heels and white stockings completed the outfit.

When she was ready, she camped around the corner from the front door and waited to ambush Cheerio. Promptly at five-thirty, the door opened. The first thing Cheerio did was shout, "Mindy! What's that elevator crap playing on the stereo for? You know I hate that!" She was looking totally secretarial in a red sweater and grey slacks and red heels. Her hair was ruffled and she had the look on her face that meant she was in a foul mood from typing letters and memos and bossing six other secretaries all day.

Mindy stepped around the corner, lifted a foot to her bottom and dabbed perfume on her ankle. Cheerio dropped her purse. Her eyes popped out of her head and rolled around on the floor. She sucked in her breath and gasped, "Mother Mary! I've died and gone to Heaven." Her face screwed up. "Is it for me this time?" she wailed.

"If you don't give me some attention tonight I'm going to explode," Mindy cooed. She sashayed over and stuck her tongue down Cheerio's throat. Cheerio whispered, "Anything," and tried to plop down right there in the hall.

Mindy led her to the bedroom. She ripped off Cheerio's sweater. Slacks. Bra. Knee-highs. Panties. She dropped to her knees in front of Cheerio. "Do you like seeing me on my knees in front of you?" she asked, kissing Cheerio's triangle and the fronts of her thighs. "Does it make you feel powerful?"

"Yes," Cheerio said. "No. Anything you say."

Mindy lowered Cheerio onto the bed and massaged her back, neck and shoulders. She gave each breast a kiss and a quick swirl of her tongue. Cheerio whimpered. Mindy kissed Cheerio's bellybutton. Cheerio's knees popped open. Mindy stroked a finger between Cheerio's legs. Cheerio was soaked already.

Sucking her finger, Mindy pranced away. "That's enough for now," she said.

"Bitch!" Cheerio groaned.

Mindy dressed Cheerio in a white slip and nothing else, like a virgin going to a sacrifice. She led her back to the great room. She poured Cheerio a glass of wine. She wedged herself into a corner of the couch and positioned Cheerio between her legs. "What are you doing?" Cheerio asked.

"Drink your wine," Mindy said. "I'm going to teach you how to work a Rubik's Cube." She ran her arms under Cheerio's breasts so she could look over her shoulder and see the puzzle. "I always start with the white. See?"

"Uh-huh," Cheerio sighed, though her eyes were closed.

Mindy managed to drop the puzzle into Cheerio's lap three or four times while she was twisting on it. She also managed to touch every inch of Cheerio's body while she was retrieving it. By the time the puzzle was half-finished, Cheerio was a quivering lump of lip-licking open-legged hussy. Mindy supposed she was, too, more or less.

"It's time for dinner," Mindy announced.

"I'm not hungry," Cheerio said hopefully, her eyes wide. "Honest."

Mindy led her to the dining room. She poured her another glass of wine. She lit candles and stuck them into ceramic holders before turning off the dining room lights. Then she served their dinner, starting with the salad, brushing her breasts or a hip or her bottom against Cheerio's neck or back or arm each time she passed. Cheerio could hardly eat from squirming in her chair.

During the steak and baked potato, Mindy said, "I had the strangest worry today."

"What?" Cheerio blurted.

"I got worried," Mindy continued, "that maybe you don't like it when I put my mouth on your side," she pointed to the ticklish spot just above her hip, "and my hand on the same spot on your other side and lick and tickle my way up, you know how I do it, up your sides to the sides of your breasts. Then I lick and tickle my way to your nipple and just when you think I'm going to take one in my mouth, my mouth and fingers change directions and work along the tops of your breasts, between your breasts, you know how I do it. Anyway, when I finally work back to your nipples, I pretend like I'm changing directions again but it's only a trick and I all of a sudden suck and tickle your nipples and you moan like you're dying."

Mindy paused and looked through her lashes. Cheerio was sawing her knife on nothing but plate. Probably because she was staring at Mindy and swallowing hard every half-second instead of paying attention to what she was doing.

Mindy purred, "I got to worrying you don't really like that at all but you're only faking. Are you faking, Cheerio, honey?"

Cheerio nodded. "I hate that," she said. "Since you brought up the subject, there's something I'm worried about, too."

"What might that be?" Mindy poked a piece of steak into her mouth. Or was it baked potato? Whatever it was, she was surprised she wasn't sliding out of her chair she felt so wet.

"You know how I put you on your side and get behind you?" Cheerio asked. "And I kiss the back of your neck and kiss my way down your back to your ass. You know how I spread your cheeks with my hands and lick all up-and-down your cheeks?" Cheerio paused to squirm in her chair, her tongue flickering across her lips.

"Know what I mean? The way I tickle your cheeks while I'm doing that? Are you faking when you say you like that?"

Mindy's knife and fork got tangled up for some reason and she managed to knock a piece of steak onto the floor. Or was it baked potato? Cheerio said, "You dropped something."

"Oh, my, so I did," Mindy agreed. She crawled under the table. Right smack dab between Cheerio's legs. She sucked Cheerio's toes. She nipped at Cheerio's feet. Calves. Knees. Thighs.

"Do you need help finding it?" Cheerio moaned.

"No, I'm finding it fine by myself, thank you," Mindy said. Her tongue might've plowed up-and-down Cheerio's moist personal spot three or four times. Maybe five or six times. Not more than seven or eight. Cheerio's knees came up and banged against the table.

"God, that was clumsy of me," Cheerio gasped.

Mindy popped back up on her side of the table. "This steak has the best flavor," she chirped brightly, licking her lips. Her cheeks felt wet. "I outdid myself tonight."

Cheerio squirmed from one side of her chair to the other. She slipped a hand under the table. Mindy said, "Get your hand out from between your legs, young lady. It's rude to grope yourself at the dinner table."

Cheerio's hand reappeared. She went back to squirming.

"I'm full," Mindy finally said.

"Stuffed," Cheerio agreed. She looked like she was sweating. She squirmed some more. "Tired, too. Let's go to bed."

Mindy pouted her lips. "You know we can't go to bed and leave all this food and dishes sitting out," she said. "You rinse and I'll wrap the leftovers and load the dishwasher."

Cheerio staggered to the sink. For some reason she kept squeezing and unsqueezing her thighs. Mindy stepped to the sink, jammed a breast against Cheerio's arm and remarked, "I bought something quite unusual today."

"What?" Cheerio blurted, turning on the water.

"A kind of lotion," Mindy said. "You put it on and it feels cool. But when you blow on it, it gets hot." She poked a hand inside Cheerio's slip and cupped a small, hard breast. "After a while I thought I'd try some on you right here," she said, tickling Cheerio's nipple. "If you don't object."

Cheerio groaned. Mindy pulled her hand out and tickled the back of a tender knee. "And here," she said. Cheerio moved her feet about a mile apart. She leaned her elbows on the counter and lowered her head toward the sink.

Mindy ran her hand up Cheerio's leg, across a silky thigh to where the hair started sprouting. The hair felt damp as the dickens. "And here," Mindy said, tweaking Cheerio's thigh. Cheerio leaned over the sink until her face was practically touching the dishes. Her breath caught in her throat. She whispered, "Stop talking about it and do me."

"Speaking of doing, you're not doing a very good job of rinsing," Mindy scolded in her best disapproving teacher's voice.

"I'm trying." Cheerio swiped weakly at a plate.

"You look tired. Maybe we better go to bed after all."

Cheerio nodded eagerly. Mindy grabbed a handful of bottom and steered Cheerio to the bedroom. But before they got there, Mindy snapped her fingers and said, "I almost forgot. How stupid. You can't go to bed yet. You haven't taken a bath."

"I'm clean, I'm clean," Cheerio protested, trying to fight to the bedroom.

But Mindy pulled her into the bathroom. She ran a nice warm bubble bath and lured Cheerio down in it. Then she promptly got on her knees and proceeded to tease every inch of Cheerio's body with a soapy washcloth so that Cheerio started practically writhing in the tub and sloshing water over the edges.

Mindy all of a sudden stopped teasing and picked up a blue hairbrush that just happened to be sitting on the edge of the tub. The hairbrush also happened to have a nice, big rounded handle. She looked around like she was confused before saying, "Hold this for me, will you? I don't have enough hands." She slid the hairbrush between Cheerio's legs. Some of the handle managed to get inside Cheerio some way. Most of the handle, actually.

Cheerio's heels popped into the air. She threw one leg over the edge of the tub, one over the soap dish and commenced going to town with the hairbrush. Mindy threw cold water in her face and said, "Stop that, you hussy. It's disgusting."

Cheerio gasped and stopped going to town with the hairbrush. "You'll pay for this," she whimpered.

"You're clean enough," Mindy said decisively. She pulled out the hairbrush, hauled Cheerio out of the tub, dried her and let her wriggle away and run into the bedroom.

Cheerio was on the bed, squirming in anticipation when Mindy strolled into the bedroom. She was also fighting to keep her hand from attacking her. Mindy stood at the foot of the bed. "Open your legs and let me see you," she ordered. "I love looking at you."

Cheerio, with a whimper, did.

"Now check this out," Mindy ordered. She let her hair down, shaking her head to spill it over her shoulders. She pulled off her top. She licked a finger and tickled her nipples, moaning softly and swaying as she did. Cheerio squirmed on the bed. Mindy said, "I can't wait to feel your mouth on my breasts, my nipples. That makes me feel so helpless." She cupped a hand under each breast, pouted her lips and said, "Do you like my breasts, Cheerio? They're not too small, are they?"

"Perfect," Cheerio blurted. "Your whole body is perfect." She squirmed some more. She licked her lips. "I want you," she whispered. "You're so pretty I could cry."

Mindy slipped her skirt down. Slowly. Cheerio gasped when she saw the white garter belt and stockings. Or did she gasp because she didn't see any panties?

Mindy propped a foot on the bed to remove her stockings. Her bottom was all but in Cheerio's face. "Leave them on," Cheerio whispered. "Please. They make your ass and legs look even sexier."

"As you wish, Love Puppy," Mindy purred. "Heels on or off?"

"On."

Mindy crawled onto the bed with her bottle of lotion. She proceeded to wallow Cheerio from one end of the bed to the other while rubbing and blowing every one of the spots she'd promised she would. And then some. Cheerio soon snatched the bottle of lotion away and reciprocated. By the time Cheerio finished, she was sitting on Mindy's chest, her knees on Mindy's shoulders, her hands pinning Mindy's arms to the bed, her crotch maybe two millimeters from Mindy's face. Close enough so Mindy could feel the heat, smell the womanly musk, a scent that was not exactly ladylike but was most definitely feminine and agonizingly alluring.

Mindy offered her tongue.

"Don't you wish," Cheerio said gleefully since she was in control, finally.

"Oh, I do, Cheerio, I do wish."

Cheerio leaned back and slipped fifteen or twenty fingers into Mindy. Mindy's heels popped into the air for some strange reason and she started doing her own going to town. When Cheerio's fingers disappeared, Mindy shivered clear down to her toes. "You're hateful," she whined. "Why are you teasing me? I'm never mean to you that way."

"You're the wildest lover I've ever had," Cheerio said, her eyes taunting. "I've never seen anyone who likes to eat girls the way you do."

Mindy squirmed. "You're such a liar," she said. "You like to eat every bit as much as I do. Maybe more. I think you're trying to use sex to dominate me."

"Admit it," Cheerio coaxed. "Admit how much you love to eat girls."

"I admit it." Mindy squirmed some more. She offered her tongue again.

"Say the words," Cheerio said.

"I won't. It's rude." Mindy struggled to get away. Not too hard, though.

"Say it." Cheerio leaned forward and swiped her sopping wet crotch across Mindy's mouth. "Say it," Cheerio insisted, a devilish look in her eye.

"I love the way women taste," Mindy said, licking her lips. "I love the way you taste. If I could, I'd eat you twenty-four hours a day and nothing else, until I finally died of starvation."

"Not good enough." Cheerio swiped her crotch across Mindy's mouth again.

"I love to eat pussy," Mindy practically gasped.

"Are you lying?" Cheerio hissed.

"I'm not. I swear I'm not." Mindy offered her tongue again.

Afterwards, they snuggled together in the dark. Mindy squeezed Cheerio as hard as she could, wishing she could crawl inside Cheerio's skin, be a complete part of her. Cheerio sighed happily and said, "That was the best combination of game-playing and mindless fucking I've had in my life."

Mindy heaved a sigh.

"I love you so much," Cheerio whispered.

"We're pregnant," Mindy whispered back. "I found out today."

Cheerio burst into tears. She kept saying, "I don't believe it. I don't believe it," over and over.

*****

Alysa blew in promptly at high noon. She looked like death warmed over. Her hair was matted down, her makeup was streaked. She stomped into the great room where Cheerio and Mindy were cuddled on the couch under a fuzzy blanket. They weren't watching TV or listening to music or anything. Just snuggling under the blanket in front of a crackling fire.

"I hope you two are happy," Alysa snapped. "Look at me. This is what sleeping in a sleazy motel and waking up without a blow-dryer or a makeup case did to me. I hope nobody I know saw me on the way here."

"You look like normal to me," Cheerio said.

Alysa eyed last night's wine bottle which was still sitting on the coffee table. She eyed Cheerio and Mindy. She put her hands on her hips, tapped a foot and stared for a long time. She finally said, "This is a nauseatingly domestic scene. I see a lot of hand movement under there. Are you two naked?"

Cheerio and Mindy both heaved sighs.

Alysa narrowed her eyes. "So tell me," she said. "Did The Formerly Frustrated Miss Cheerio get her some loving last night?"

Cheerio practically chortled.

"I see," Alysa said, with a thoughtful expression. "So I'm safe in assuming The Formerly Frustrated Miss Mindy got her some loving as well?"

Mindy heaved another sigh.

"Can The Still Frustrated Miss Alysa join you two under that blanket?"

"Pervert!" Cheerio said.

Alysa stamped a foot. "I want some loving, too!" she wailed.

"Go out and find some," Cheerio said. "When has that been a problem for you?"

Alysa dropped down into a chair. She looked depressed all of a sudden. "I'm sick of come-and-go relationships," she said. "I want to find someone I can live happy ever after with. You two and your relatively successful domesticity have inspired me."

Mindy traced a fingernail up Cheerio's thigh, feeling sorry for Alysa, but she didn't know what she could do. Cheerio shifted and poked her tongue into Mindy's mouth. Alysa said, "I'm going to sit here all day so you two can't give in to your hormones."

"We're pregnant," Cheerio announced.

Alysa's mouth dropped open. "No lie?" she asked in awe.

"Doctor-certified," Mindy said. "I've been released to an obstetrician. My first appointment is Monday afternoon. Her name is Donnie Marks. The Gay Information Line referred me to her."

"Congratulations!" Alysa slapped her thighs. "Is that what you say to an expectant mother?"

"*Mothers*," Cheerio corrected.

"Who's the father?" Alysa asked. "You know what I mean."

"I don't know much," Mindy said. "I know he's a WASP and a promising medical student. That's about it."

"Do tell," Alysa said, pursing her lips. "A math mother and a doctor father. Probably turn out with an I.Q. somewhere between a beet and a cabbage."

"Good-bye, Mary," Cheerio said firmly. She closed her eyes and burrowed farther under the blanket.

Alysa had a disgusted look on her face. "I'm going to bed," she said. "Alone. Again." She stomped out.

CHAPTER 9

"You're doing wonderfully," Dr. Marks beamed, removing the practically frigid stethoscope from Mindy's belly. Dr. Marks was a tiny brunette with blue eyes. "Your second trimester shouldn't be any problem. You're as healthy as a horse." Her mouth quirked at the corners like it always did when she was teasing. "You're prime breeding stock."

"All right!" Mindy declared, feeling motherly and hormone-charged and productive. Or reproductive, actually. She slipped her size elevens out of the stirrups and sat up. It was sure a lot more pleasant crawling onto a table and spreading her legs for a woman doctor than a man doctor.

"I don't have anything to tell you," Dr. Marks said, scribbling something in Mindy's file. Mindy's file was about a foot thick, she supposed because she'd been artificially "speculated." "Stick with your vitamins and your exercises. Get plenty of rest. Try to get off your feet whenever possible." She laughed. "I know that's hard for a teacher, but do your best."

Mindy gave her a mock salute, set a date for her next appointment and said good-bye. When she got to the outer office, she stopped at the receptionist's desk and pulled out her checkbook. The waiting room was jammed with swollen preggies and squalling children and harried-looking mothers, since Dr. Marks had a partner who was a pediatrician.

"Are we paying by check today?" the blond receptionist bubbled to Mindy.

"If I have to," Mindy grumbled. She leaned close to the receptionist and whispered, "Although I still think lesbian doctors should see lesbian patients for free."

The receptionist snickered and whispered back confidentially, "Dykes get hungry, too," she added. "Dykes have bills to pay."

*****

Mindy met Tanika Kenson during her junior year in college. Tanika was an inky-black woman, and had an absolutely gorgeous bottom and heavy, sensual-looking lips. She was an eighteen-year-old freshman. Mindy went head-over-heels as soon as she saw Tanika, so she brazenly asked for a date and Tanika accepted. They made love on the second date, in the back seat of Mindy's car at the drive-in. Tanika was a virgin, but Mindy and her head-over-heels lust took care of that problem in just a few seconds. Tanika turned out, once she lost her maidenhead, to be the most eager lover Mindy had ever taken. Tanika was also the first multiorgasmic lover Mindy had taken up to that point in her life. Tanika would come and come until the cows came home. It made Mindy like something wild, made her feel like God's gift to the female orgasm.

Years later, Mindy still felt bummed every time she thought about Tanika because, after eight weeks, Mindy had broken Tanika's heart by falling madly in love with a beanpole blond with big blue eyes named Kelli—Mindy had always been a pushover for beanpole blonds with blue eyes. When Mindy dropped her bombshell, Tanika cried because she was humiliated over being dumped for a beanpole blond with blue eyes. Mindy tried to explain that broken hearts were part of going head-over-heels and Tanika would survive. Tanika made a fist and punched Mindy in the stomach and said her first was the one she'd never forget and she'd also never forget to hate Mindy for as long as she lived.

Six weeks later, Kelli dumped Mindy for another beanpole blond with blue eyes named Trish, leaving Mindy wondering just what the dickens was going on in the world when everyone wanted beanpole blonds with blue eyes. She thought it didn't seem fair that two beanpole blonds with blue eyes should fall madly in love with each other when there were only so many beanpole blonds with blue eyes to be had.

Mindy promptly went to Tanika's dorm room and tried to tiptoe her way back between Tanika's legs. But before Mindy could even say one word, Tanika bellowed, "I have a new lover named Bess. She's blond and has blue eyes," and slammed the door in Mindy's face, leaving Mindy to ponder the fact that Tanika had a lover and Bess had a lover and Kelli had a lover and Trish had a lover, while all Mindy had was a soapy washcloth, a petulant attitude and a depression stupor that defied description.

Shandra Tillmon closely reminded Mindy of Tanika. Shandra was also an inky-black woman in her mid-twenties. She was short, plump and energetic and had the same gorgeous bottom and heavy, sensual-looking lips. Besides having a gorgeous bottom, Shandra Tillmon also had a downtown law office she shared with a blond accountant named Barry Wilton. Their office was on the fourth floor of a rickety old building. To get there you had to pay a dollar to park two blocks away, walk past a line of bus stops, towering office buildings, hot dog stands and trash-cluttered alleys.

Shandra's office had a battered pressed-wood desk that reminded Mindy of the one she had at school. Her desk was piled with papers and books and a fistful of Bic pens in an apple sauce can and a half-eaten peanut butter sandwich resting on a brown paper sack and three diet Coke cans and several crumpled-up potato chip packages.

Shandra was wearing a well-tailored grey suit, a white silk blouse, and neat black pumps. She bustled into the office, pushed up her sleeves, collapsed into her chair and said, "Whew! Fridays are wild around here. It's the day the docket is heaviest at court." She picked up the half-eaten peanut butter sandwich, took a nibble and set it back down. Then she picked up one of the diet Coke cans, shook it, tossed it into a metal trash can with a 'bang,' picked up another one and took a quick sip.

"I'm three and a half months pregnant," Mindy said.

"Girlfriend!" Shandra exclaimed, her eyes shining. She had darling, liquid-brown eyes. "Are you excited?"

"Of course." Mindy paused while Shandra burrowed around her desk. After Shandra finished burrowing and pulled out a legal pad, Mindy said, "I'm not getting married."

"And why should you if you don't want to?" Shandra leaned back in her chair with a squeak.

Mindy crossed her legs. "When I talked to you six months ago, you said you'd be interested in helping me if I got in trouble with the school board."

Shandra laughed. She had a deep reassuring laugh, like the things that happened in life were a bunch of folderol and nothing at all to get worried over. "I'm ready to do the humpty-hump with the school board right now," she said. "All I need is the word from you."

"I'd rather be more defensive," Mindy said. "If they leave me alone I'll leave them alone."

"Sure." Shandra pressed her fingertips together. She all of a sudden snapped her fingers and jumped up to pace around behind her desk. "This double-standard garbage has to end," she declared. "It's high time it did. I'm just the woman to help it along the way." She stopped pacing and studied Mindy. "Maybe we can get a class action suit going," she said. "Do you know any teachers who've been discriminated against because they had a baby out of wedlock?"

"No," Mindy said. "There's the matter of my lesbianism to consider, too."

"Oh." Shandra chewed on a thumbnail. "I appreciate your honesty. You have to be honest with me about everything or I can't help you." She flopped down in her chair. She had a funny look on her face. An excited look more than anything. "The school board wouldn't be thrilled to know you're a lesbian," she mused, almost like she was talking to herself.

"I haven't exactly discussed it with them, but I doubt they'd jump for joy."

"Do you want to introduce that as part of your case?" Shandra asked, locking eyes with Mindy. "If you do, you might want to talk to a lawyer more familiar with gay rights. I can refer you to several prominent ones."

"No, thank you," Mindy replied. "I don't want to be a torchbearer for all lesbians. There are women far more capable than me who can do that. Women more financially secure."

Shandra studied Mindy for several seconds. "I hear you," Shandra finally said. "Low-key's the word." She hopped out of her chair and bounced around the office, clapping her hands and laughing. She stopped all of a sudden and declared, "I'm sorry. I'm not laughing at you. I'm only turned on by this case."

Shandra grabbed a chair, pulled it next to Mindy's and continued, "You're a once in a lifetime case for me. I usually get drunk drivers, dopers, burglars, divorce cases in here. What you're talking about is a chance to challenge some of the bad things in the system. Cases like yours are why I went to law school."

"Well," Mindy offered. She didn't know what else to say.

"You're the first white person to sit in that chair in my two years of practice," Shandra said. Her eyes turned hard. Angry-looking maybe. "Nobody thinks a nappy-headed black girl from the north side projects can do the job." She jumped up. She slapped her hands on her desk with both hands. Potato chip wrappers flew into the air. "They're wrong!" she cried. "I want your case. Not because I think we can win, although I think we can. But because it's right. My time will be free. The only cost to you will be filing fees and the like. I'll go to the wall for you. I give you my word on that. Please say you'll let me represent you."

"That's what I'm here for," Mindy agreed, offering her hand.

Shandra broke into a smile. Her eyes went back to shining. She shook hands. The other hand she thrust into the air and made a fist. "Yes!" she exclaimed. "Yes-yes-yes!"

Mindy said good-bye and left. She promptly got caught in the Friday afternoon rush hour, which certainly made her day.

******

"Fine," Mindy said angrily. "If you want me out of my sisters' lives, then you want me out of your lives, too. That's the only way I can look at things." She slammed the phone down without bothering to say good-bye.

Cheerio snapped a fireplace match. The gas starter went 'whoosh!' She squatted and watched the logs catch hold. The flames cast a flickering light across her face and made her hair and eyebrows look almost white. Her hair was in stubby pigtails that were practically too cute for words.

"I don't know what happened," Mindy remarked, a hurt look on her face. "Things just snowballed all of a sudden. I thought if I was calm and reasonable with them they'd understand. I suppose I thought I could pull it off, even though hardly anybody I know has been able to. Am I arrogant or what?"

"Nobody likes hearing their daughter's a dyke," Cheerio commiserated. "Want to be alone so you can cry?"

"I don't feel like crying right now."

Cheerio moved to the couch. She got on her knees beside Mindy and massaged Mindy's shoulders and nuzzled her neck. "Give them some time," Cheerio murmured. "It took a while for my parents to get used to it. Mom finally said that out of eight kids she didn't guess one homo was such bad odds."

Daddy and Mother had sounded like the same old Mother and Daddy when Mindy first called. She got them both on the phone at the same time and chatted about the weather and so forth before dropping her bombshell and telling them she was pregnant through an artificial insemination. Good old J.D. and Rachel Brinson promptly started spouting religious dogma about how conception was something within God's realm and man should stay out of it. To hear them tell it, they would've preferred Mindy sleep with every man in town because getting pregnant that way would be natural, albeit whorish.

And when Mindy told them she didn't consider herself an unwed mother because she was married to Cheerio? Laws! They didn't say a word for at least five full minutes. Long enough for Mindy to start worrying that they'd dropped dead from his-and-her heart attacks. When the silence finally ended, Daddy went to whipping up an asinine gale with his tongue, yelling something about not wanting to hear such talk because marriage was *A Holy Institution* and for two girls to claim they were married was blasphemy. Mindy's temper and blood pressure both went through the roof and she promptly told Daddy to kiss her ass. She heard the sound of him dropping his teeth all the way from Kentucky.

Just then, Alysa pranced into the great room, wearing skin, hair and nothing else. Her hair was teased to next week, her stage makeup was thick, and she was scratching the dickens out of her crotch with her right hand. Her left arm was loaded with dirty clothes. She stopped and eyed the way Cheerio and Mindy were acting on the couch.

"Alysa—" Mindy began.

"I know, I know," Alysa said. "Get out. I recognize a personal moment when I see one." She turned to leave.

"I was only going to say your breakfast is in the oven," Mindy said. "There's also two dozen fresh-baked biscuits. I thought you could take some to the other women in the band tonight to share during a break."

"Thanks," Alysa said flashing a smile. She pointed to the clothes in her left arm. "Please, Miss Mindy," she wheedled prettily. "Could you?"

"Toss them in the laundry room," Mindy said, pretending to be disgusted, when she really wasn't. "I'll do them sometime before you leave. Tomorrow. Or Sunday."

"You're a doll." Alysa again flashed the dazzling smile that had broken women's hearts all over the country. She pointed to the plate of cookies on the coffee table. "Are those some of your great and famous homemade chocolate chip cookies?" she asked yearningly.

Mindy nodded. "I wrapped some for you. They're in the oven with your breakfast. There's two dozen extra you can take to work tonight, too. They're in the Tupperware bowl on the kitchen counter."

Alysa's face lit up. "I'd kill for your chocolate chip cookies when they're still warm," she said. She raced into the kitchen like a spoiled little kid, which she pretty much was. Mindy called, "Drink some orange juice with your breakfast instead of soda or beer. There's some in the refrigerator."

"Yes, Mother," Alysa said, sounding disgusted now that she was through manipulating.

Cheerio hopped off the couch. She spread a multicolored afghan on the floor in front of the fireplace. She patted a spot in the center of the afghan and said, "Down here. I'll massage your back and we'll do your stretching and exercising."

Mindy stretched out and stared at the fire. Knead, knead, knead went Cheerio's fingers. After Mindy told Daddy to kiss her ass, Mother went to babbling something about a book she'd read not long after Mindy and Cheerio bought their house, causing Mindy to realize Mother already knew about Mindy's lesbianism, or at least suspected, so why was Mother acting so shocked?

Mother said the book she read taught her everything there was to learn about the 'liking girls thing' so she didn't need to talk about it with Mindy. Then Mother went to babbling about Michelle Beth Warton and how she used to prance around in front of the local army base selling herself to GI's for twenty-five dollars a pop so she could pay for the snazzy red Corvette she catted around in. Mindy had wondered aloud what prostitution had to do with lesbianism. Mother said something along the lines of how daughters sometimes made their parents' lives miserable. Mindy promptly told Mother she was more than welcome to kiss her ass right after Daddy got through kissing it.

Mother had cried and said, "Mindy, sometimes I feel like such a failure. It's hard for me to accept that I've failed as a mother. Failed you, my husband, my God." Her voice cracked. "Especially when I had so much to work with."

Cheerio's fingers stopped going knead-knead-knead. She hopped to her feet. "On your back," she ordered, tossing a pillow down for Mindy to rest on. "Give me your left foot."

Mindy obeyed. Cheerio stretched Mindy's left leg all the way up. And up. And up. "Damn," Cheerio grunted. "Your legs are unreal."

"Poke a paintbrush in my toes and I'll paint the ceiling," Mindy said. Mother had sobbed, "How am I going to live with my failure?"

Alysa walked back in, carrying a tray with her breakfast. There was a glass of wine sitting on her tray where a glass of orange juice should've been. "Can I sit in here?" she asked, with a friendly expression. "I hate to eat alone. You know me." She flashed her brilliant smile.

"That's fine, sweetie," Mindy said. "If it makes you happy."

Mother had said, "I've prayed for you every day for years, but it never helps. You'll never change."

"Right leg," Cheerio grunted, depositing Mindy's left leg on the floor. Cheerio was practically sweating. Mindy supposed the exercises did more for Cheerio than Mindy. All the stretching and exercising was supposed to do something about making it easier to squirt out a baby when the time came. Mindy wasn't real sure how or why. Cheerio was the exercise expert.

Alysa plopped into a chair, curled her legs under herself and took a bite of bacon. She always ate in dainty, nibbling bites. It was darling, in a childlike sort of way. Spike promptly camped out in front of Alysa, licking her lips and looking up with a mournful expression until Alysa gave her a piece of bacon. Spike hunkered down and went to growling and ripping at the bacon with her miniature fangs.

"Both legs," Cheerio ordered.

"Hhmmm?" Mindy asked because somewhere along the line she'd gotten sidetracked. Mostly from staring at Alysa's unshaven legs and the black hair sprouting under her arms and the cobra tattoo on her left thigh. She had a second tattoo on her right breast, of a rose. Alysa flopped her legs open so Mindy could get a real good look at what she was gawking at.

"My breakfast is great," Alysa said in a purring voice. "I see the way you're looking at it. Slide over here and I'll let you do more than look. Your tongue's halfway here. I can almost feel it on my tray."

Mindy felt embarrassed. But she kept gawking. Alysa had the hairiest crotch this side of anywhere. And her breasts were absolutely heavenly.

"Looks good, doesn't it?" Alysa cooed, licking butter from a biscuit. Slowly.

"God-damn dyke bitch!" Cheerio snapped.

"You know it looks good," Mindy said. "That must be why you're flaunting it in front of me. You know Cheerio won't let me eat anything like that. It's not on my diet."

Cheerio bent over and gave Mindy's bottom a ringing slap. Her eyes were probing and questioning and more than a little angry-looking. Mindy teased, "Beat me until I cry, Cheerio. The more you beat me the more I love you."

Cheerio leaned down and poked her tongue into Mindy's mouth. Mindy said, "Let's finish exercising in bed," loud enough for Alysa to hear.

Cheerio's 'bite my bottom' smile appeared on her face. She gave Alysa the finger before pushing both Mindy's legs toward the ceiling. Or the moon, actually.

"This is better than great," Alysa said, biting into a cookie. She rolled her eyes and moaned, "Uummm," licking chocolate off her lips. Slowly. Her mocking eyes bored into Mindy's. Her legs opened wider.

"It does look sweet," Mindy said.

"I know what you're doing!" Cheerio snapped. "You're paying me back for the flirting I did with her while you were running around with guys. I don't like it, god-dammit. I want you to know that."

"You're right. I'm sorry," Mindy said. Daddy had shouted, "Why are you doing this to your mother? What has she done to deserve this?" He had sounded absolutely self-righteous. Mindy had closed her eyes and pictured him hitching up his pants and arching his eyebrows like he always did when he was absolutely self-righteous.

"Close your legs, Alysa," Cheerio hissed, looking irritated. "If an outsider heard you, they'd think you were serious about all this."

"Who says I'm not?" Alysa asked coyly, licking on her cookie. "I'm offering to share my breakfast with you, too, Cheerio Monroe. Both of you at the same time. One at a time. I don't care."

"Why do you look so grim, Cheerio?" Mindy asked. "Alysa's just horsing around like she always does. And I already apologized."

"Have either of you taken part in group sex before?" Alysa cooed.

"Mother Mary!" Cheerio exclaimed. "Do your sit-ups!"

"Oh, I hate those," Mindy groaned.

"They're good for your back and abdomen," Cheerio said, positioning Mindy for her mandatory fifteen sit-ups.

"I love you," Alysa sighed without indicating exactly who she loved. Probably the cookie she was still licking.

"It's waist-deep and rising," Cheerio growled, rolling her eyes.

"Five...six...seven," Mindy puffed. Mother had sobbed, "God forgive me, but I hate everything connected to this. I don't want it to be true about you. I don't want the whispers I hear about you at the grocery store to be true." Mindy had shrieked, "People are gossiping about me at the grocery store?" As if it mattered what anyone in Hopkinsville, Kentucky said or did. But screaming about the people at the grocery store seemed easier than facing Mother's sense of failure and shame.

"Fifteen," Cheerio counted. "Good girl! Leg lifts now." She rolled Mindy onto her side and helped get the leg lifts going.

"Easy. I'm not a wishbone," Mindy grunted. Mother had sobbed, "Yes, they talk about you at the grocery store. They say you're...different. Queer. They say it's a shame you want to be that way because you're beautiful and could have any boy you want."

Alysa glided to the coffee table. She bent a knee, cocked a hip and modeled the back view of her bottom and legs as she opened the box of Whitman's candy Mindy had bought that afternoon. It was a gorgeous pair of legs and bottom Alysa was modeling. Firm and smooth and shapely. She squished a piece of candy with her thumb, made a face and squished another piece. She popped the second piece into her mouth. She was a hard-core candy-squisher. Cheerio was, too. Every box of candy Mindy brought home ended up squished to death inside of an hour or two.

"Alysa," Mindy said.

"Melinda Sue, darling." Alysa turned around. Her lips were slightly parted, her eyes hooded, she had a sensual expression on her face. Mindy couldn't help wondering if Alysa really was excited. From all the exercising maybe. Mindy was only dressed in a flimsy pink wrap, after all, and was probably flashing everything she had. It was exciting in a strangely perverted sort of way to be fanning the fires in a beautiful woman right in front of her lover.

"Other leg," Cheerio said, rolling Mindy over. Alysa glided around to make eye contact with Mindy.

"I came out to my parents tonight," Mindy said.

"It was a drag when I came out to my folks," Alysa said, folding both her arms under her breasts. Her nipples looked hard. She cocked a hip, modeling the front view of what she had to offer. The front view was as gorgeous as the back. "They kicked me out of the house," Alysa continued. "After I stayed away for a while, they changed to where they can tolerate me. That's all you can hope for, I guess. How did yours take it?"

"Daddy said something has gone wrong with me. He ordered me to keep away from my sisters. No letters, no calls. Nothing. He said I might corrupt them."

"Yeah, like you're contagious," Alysa sneered. Her eyes flashed.

"I don't understand how he could say something like that," Mindy said. "If the love I feel for my sisters could possible corrupt them, then I'm guilty. I've corrupted the hell out of them. I asked him what exactly *happened* to me? I told him I've never been happier in my life. Why would that be someone's fault? That seems stupid to me. I can't believe he's trying to blame me because he's miserable because I'm happy. If that makes any sense."

"Up against the wall," Cheerio ordered. She helped Mindy up, then jammed her against the wall and said, "Your posture's been for crap lately. Remember what Dr. Marks told you? How important posture is? I don't want to see any light between your back and the wall. Work on your breathing, too."

"What reason could he have for taking my sisters away?" Mindy asked, lifting her right knee as high as she could. "What does he think I'd do to them? Take them to bed?"

"Who knows?" Alysa asked with a shrug.

"The drugs have to go," Mindy said out of the blue, switching to her left knee.

Alysa's eyes widened. She put on her innocent face and shook her head. "I haven't— she began.

"Don't bother lying," Mindy said. "Bringing drugs into this house and hiding them in your room has to end. There's no telling when the police will be watching you. They'd love to arrest the lead guitar player for a lesbian group as famous as Silky Wet. That would involve all of us."

"I know you're upset about your parents," Alysa reasoned. "But there's no need to take it out on me."

"I'm not taking anything out on you. The drugs go or you go. I'm stating facts."

You Light The Fire

"You've ruined everything!" Alysa all of a sudden shouted, causing wide-eyed Cheerio to back up two or three steps. With good reason. Alysa looked mad enough to kill, although it was hard to take her seriously when she was only wearing skin, hair and nothing else. "I was feeling close to you, like part of this household because you made me breakfast and you've talked to me about your problems and included me in your happy things, like your exercising. I felt like I was wanted and I belonged, even if I'm not wanted sexually. You've ruined the feelings I had."

"I didn't mean to," Mindy said, trying to touch Alysa's arm.

Alysa backed away. "I won't have my personal actions dictated by a Hitler with tits!" she shouted, her eyes flashing. She stomped back to her bedroom. She stomped back through the house in a minute, dressed in one of her patented white/black velvet/leather outfits. She went into the kitchen. When she reappeared, she was hugging the Tupperware bowl of cookies and the package of biscuits in both her arms. "I'll move my things when I get back from Hawaii!" she barked before slamming the front door.

"Was that melodramatic or what!" Mindy exclaimed. She looked at Cheerio. Cheerio's face was practically deathly white, she was wringing the dickens out of her sweat shirt with both hands.

"What are you going to do?" Cheerio blurted.

"About what?"

"Me," Cheerio squeaked. "First your parents. Then Alysa. Am I the next one you kick out of your life tonight?"

"What reason would I have for doing that?"

"A bunch of reasons," Cheerio croaked. She looked at Mindy with terrified eyes and twisted harder on her grey sweatshirt. Mindy moved to her and gave the insecure little thing a sloppy kiss.

"Where would I find a beanpole blond with huge blue eyes to replace you?" Mindy whispered after the sloppy kiss. "There's precious few of you around." She slipped a hand between Cheerio's toasty-warm thighs and tweaked her crotch. Then she said, "I feel like a total jock. I think I'll shower and lotion my legs and watch TV. There's a Bogart and Bacall movie on later I want to see, if you don't mind. Maybe I'll put on something soft and frilly after my shower. Would my white baby-doll please you?"

"Uh-huh," Cheerio said, a goofy grin and a relieved expression on her face.

"Want to join me?" Mindy asked.

"For the shower or the movie?"

"Both."

"Can we have popcorn?"

"With a shower? How perverted." Mindy walked into the bathroom. Cheerio was right on her heels.

When the phone rang at eleven, they were snuggled on the couch under a blanket in front of a blazing fire. Mindy reached around Cheerio to answer it and heard Alysa shouting, "Cheerio! Has that stone-cold bitch cooled down yet?" Voices murmured and music blared in the background.

"Do I sound like Cheerio?" Mindy asked huffily.

"Jesus," Alysa groaned. "You two sweet peas have been married so long I can't tell one of your Southern accents from the other. How long have you been together?"

"Going on five years," Mindy said. "You should know that. We invited you to the party we're planning."

"You've got my tits in a wringer," Alysa sighed. "I don't want to leave. I'm in love with you two."

"I see."

"Why doesn't anyone believe me when I say I love them?" Alysa practically wailed. "Do you think people don't see me as sincere?"

"I won't answer that," Mindy said. "But you know we love you, too. You also know you can stay here forever if you want. But you understand the conditions."

"No smoke, no blow around the house."

"No kidding."

Alysa heaved a sigh. "What if I eventually meet someone I can be happy ever after with?" she asked. "How will I find the heart to leave you two?"

"You don't have to," Mindy said. "Move her in here. We'll be happy to have her."

"No shit? You'd do that for me?"

Mindy laughed. "Hey, us women-lovin'-women have to stick together."

"I love you, Mindy!" Alysa bellowed over the background noise. "I put my rent money in an envelope on my dresser before I left. Catch you on the flip side." The phone went click.

Mindy wrapped her arms around Cheerio. Cheerio murmured something unintelligible. She was half-asleep, not being what you'd call a hard-core Bogart and Bacall fan. Mindy whispered, "If you'll wake up I'll make it worth your while, sweetheart."

"I'm awake. I think."

Mindy slipped a hand between Cheerio's thighs, marveling yet again how eagerly Cheerio shifted and opened herself up to accept the probing. Cheerio pushed her hands under Mindy's baby-doll.

"Don't," Mindy begged. "I don't want you to see my stomach. I'm fat."

"Dumb-ass," Cheerio said, tugging at Mindy's top. "I sleep with you every night. I shower with you every day. I want to see you. It's *our* baby growing in your belly, and I love both of you." She kissed all around Mindy's stomach.

"Let's spend the night here in front of the fire," Mindy practically whimpered. "Right here in our cocoon on the couch. I feel so warm and contented and safe with you. I don't ever want to move."

CHAPTER 10

"I peeked in Alysa's room when I got home from work," Mindy said thoughtfully. "She was in bed with a fawn."

"Huh?" Cheerio sneaked a hunk of salmon cake to Spike. Mindy snapped, "Don't feed the dog at the table. It irritates the dickens out of me." Cheerio said, "Okay," and dropped some more salmon cake into Spike's mouth.

"Did you hear what I said?" Mindy asked. "About Alysa and not the dog? It's obvious you didn't hear what I said about the dog." Cheerio grinned down at Spike. Mindy said, "I saw Alysa in bed with a fawn. I don't know what else to call the creature she was sleeping with." She paused, waiting for a response. Nothing. She continued: "The creature Alysa is sleeping with is an exquisite shade of tawny brown, and has long black hair and a great pair of legs. She also has a blue suitcase with 'Fawn' monogrammed on it beneath the handle."

"Slut," Cheerio said, giving Spike a bite of cottage cheese. Spike made a sour face and spit it on the floor, causing Mindy to feel murderous. Cheerio whispered confidentially, "I don't blame you. I hate the shit, too."

"I'm not a slut," Mindy protested. "I'm completely happy with you. But I can still appreciate a great pair of legs when I see them. The fawn I saw in bed with Alysa has an exquisite bottom, too. Nice and full and rounded."

"Slut," Cheerio repeated. "I saw what you tried to do with the Greeson's cocker spaniel when I took you walking this evening. I guess you'll spread those hairy little legs for any guy that pants by."

Mindy heaved a sigh. She started clearing the table and rinsing dishes to put in the washer. Cheerio walked to the sink, lifted Mindy's maternity dress and pinched her bottom. "Leave me alone," Mindy said in mock disgust. "You don't listen to anything I say any more."

"So Alysa brought a gash-ette home with her," Cheerio said. "What do you want me to do?"

"Nothing," Mindy pouted. "I just like to gossip about people. The least you could do is have the courtesy to gossip back."

Cheerio laughed and gave Mindy's bottom a ringing slap. Mindy said, "Eat me." Cheerio licked her lips and walked into the great room.

Mindy had just finished cleaning the kitchen when she heard water running and voices murmuring on the other side of the house. She decided to make Alysa's first night home special by fixing an omelette, so she took eggs and tomatoes and green onions and jalapeno peppers and cheese and picante sauce out of the refrigerator. She didn't know if fawns liked omelettes, but she figured if this particular fawn didn't like omelettes, then this particular fawn could fix her own breakfast. After she tossed everything into the skillet she started her floured potato-cakes frying in another skillet and then went to work on a plate of buttered toast. Alysa devoured toast by the ton.

Just as she flipped her omelette, she heard Cheerio and Alysa swapping insults in the great room.

Cheerio asked, "Who's the kid? Does her ma-ma know where she is?" in a challenging tone of voice.

Alysa sassily replied, "Mindy told me if I met someone special I could bring her home. She's twenty-one, for your information. I looked at her driver's license before I bedded her."

Cheerio sneered, "Twenty-one days or twenty-one months?"

Alysa snapped, "Your lover is younger than you."

133

Cheerio retorted, "She's not ten years younger. She's twenty-seven and I'm only thirty-two."

And then Alysa and her fawn walked into the kitchen. Mindy looked past Alysa at the fawn, her eyes filling with skintight white jeans and a pink halter top and pink stiletto heels and waist-length black hair and a turned-up nose. The fawn sat down at the table shyly, folded her hands in her lap, her face lowered bashfully.

Cheerio appeared in the door, clutching Spike to her neck. She arched her eyebrows and nodded toward Alysa's fawn, her expression saying *yum-yum*. Mindy divided the omelette in two, slid it onto plates, added a potato cake and a slice of tomato to each plate, picked up the toast and moved to the table at the speed of waddle. She couldn't help noticing how much softer around her eyes Alysa looked. She looked like she was about to pop from pride and love.

"You walk like a duck with hemorrhoids," Cheerio remarked. She practically chortled at her own joke. Spike went yap-yap, since she played the straight girl in The Cheerio Monroe Comedy Show.

"Quack-quack," Mindy said, wondering if she felt like giving Cheerio a shot in the chops. "Please don't mention hemorrhoids to me." She docked herself at a chair to get off her feet for a while.

"This is Fawn Yamato," Alysa said. "Fawn, this is Mindy Brinson." Fawn pressed her mouth to Alysa's ear and whispered. Alysa laughed. Fawn focused a luminous pair of almond-shaped black eyes on Mindy, and blinked once, slowly, just like a real fawn. "I told her you were pregnant," Alysa explained. "But she's noticed you're *real* pregnant. I'm shocked, too. You've sure ballooned since the last time I saw you."

"So that's what's wrong with me!" Mindy clapped a hand to her forehead. "I was beginning to worry I had a stomach tumor. Thanks for saving me a trip to the doctor."

"I was bisexual at one time," Fawn said in a whispery voice. "I was unhappy until I finally admitted to myself I'm a pure lesbian. Now I'm proud of who I am." She blinked again, slowly.

Cheerio snickered and rolled her eyes. Mindy didn't say anything, although her eyebrows practically catapulted through the roof. Alysa patted Fawn's hand and said, "Doll, everyone here's as comfortably lesbian as the next guy."

"I talk too much sometimes," Fawn said. Her face disappeared, and she presented a perfect part bracketed by shiny black hair. "I'm sorry. Can we start over? I'd hate for a woman as pretty as you to dislike me."

"Isn't she cute," Alysa cooed. "Don't you just love her?"

"If only she wasn't so closemouthed," Cheerio said. Alysa shot Cheerio a dirty look. Mindy hoisted anchor, waddled to the sink to clean her mess and said, "How was your road trip? I've never been to Hawaii. Is it nice?" She was thinking, *I could sure use a five month trip to Hawaii right about now.*

"Nice doesn't describe it," Alysa sighed.

"Hawaii is my home," Fawn said, her face re-appearing. She had a subdued expression. "I was born on Kauai. I can tell you anything you want to know." She picked up her fork, took a bite of omelette and put her fork back on her plate.

"That would be nice," Mindy said, placing a skillet in the dishwasher.

"This omelette is delicious," Fawn said. "You're an excellent cook." She picked up her fork, took a bite of omelette and put her fork back down.

Mindy heaved a sigh. How was she supposed to be miffed at someone who gushed compliments like they were about to be outlawed? She waddled back to the table, plunked herself down and asked, "What kind of work do you do, Fawn?"

Fawn flashed a smile. "I'm a singer," she said shyly. "I was performing at an amateur night competition in Honolulu when Alysa discovered me. She invited me to audition for her band, so here I am. I'm thrilled. Silky Wet is the first professional band I've performed with." She looked at Cheerio. "Alysa told me you used to sing professionally, and cut an album one time. Maybe you could listen to me and give me your opinion since I'm just starting out and you've already been there and quit."

Cheerio bristled noticeably. "Sure," she said. She abruptly added, "I have something to do," and disappeared.

Fawn's face flushed. She lowered her face and presented her part again. Mindy said comfortingly, "I remember when I first moved to Tulsa and met Cheerio and Alysa. I could barely open my mouth without making someone mad." She patted Fawn's hand comfortingly.

Fawn lifted her face and smiled. She all of a sudden clutched Mindy's hand and blurted, "I about died on the airplane flying here! It was my first time!"

Mindy laughed and squeezed her hand.

"Time to go," Alysa said, gently brushing at Fawn's hair.

Fawn gulped. "I'm *so* nervous," she squeaked, wiping her hands on her jeans. "Alysa told me I only get to sing two songs in the second set and two more in the fourth, since it's my first professional appearance. I'll get my purse." She bolted from the table.

"I love her," Alysa said simply, watching Fawn go. "So Mindy, are you still working?"

"I have to work until I drop my foal," Mindy confided. "Financial reasons, you know."

*****

Spike jumped into Mindy's lap, yapped, growled and finally stretched out. Mindy tickled her ears. Spike heaved a sigh and closed her eyes. Spike had developed an affinity for sleeping in Mindy's lap the last few weeks. Mindy supposed it was because Spike could hear the baby's heart beating and her own mothering instincts got aroused.

Mindy leaned her head back and closed her eyes. It was in her sixth month, in February, when she couldn't hide her condition inside baggy sweaters and loose dresses anymore, that she was ordered to report to her principal's office. He announced that she was a bad role model for her students, so she was being transferred to central office the next day. She would remain there for the rest of the school term, working in the cumulative records office. Mindy argued herself blue in the face, sounding like she was trying to talk the hangman out of throwing the lever.

"I'm being discriminated against because I'm a woman," she said angrily. "I'm being punished over my looks, while a man who is an unwed expectant father would never be punished over his looks. A man would be allowed to stay in the classroom."

"You can't look at a man and tell he's an expectant father," Mr. Stone countered.

"You're admitting I'm being punished because of my looks," Mindy said. "By transferring me, you're teaching the kids a bad lesson. You're teaching them a woman is shameful unless she has a man by her side to give validation to everything she does. Leaving me with my kids teaches them a better lesson. It teaches them a woman can be a person all by herself."

"I didn't think you'd take it this way," Mr. Stone said, sounding annoyed. "Most teachers would welcome a chance to get away from the students and still get paid. It's obvious you're in the wrong mental state for teaching. I'm relieving you of your duties as of this minute. Report for your new assignment in the morning."

"Yes, sir," Mindy said, almost saluting. She left, feeling frustrated enough to chew bark off a tree. The first thing she did when she got home was call Shandra and say, "I just got transferred away from my kids and I'm pissed."

"So what's the word?" Shandra asked, sounding like she was holding her breath.

"Go."

The next morning, Shandra promptly filed a sex discrimination lawsuit against the school board, asking for three hundred thousand dollars in punitive damages and two hundred thousand for mental anguish. She also filed for a preliminary injunction against the school board, asking that the transfer be blocked until a hearing could be held, arguing the school board was acting in an arbitrarily oppressive manner and causing injury to Mindy based on a fuzzy moral turpitude contract clause.

The phone started ringing off the hook at five that afternoon with reporters wanting to arrange an interview to get the inside scoop. Mindy referred five or six to Shandra so Shandra could tell them, "No comment." She finally got disgusted and unplugged the phone at six-thirty. Cheerio said, "We're outta here until things cool down. Sherry and Jo will put us up for as long as it takes."

"I'll be glad when our fifteen minutes of fame is over," Mindy said tiredly.

Two days later, wearing a hat and a black veil to hide her face from the mob of shutterbugs camped out in front of the school, Mindy walked back into her classroom, with her head held high and a triumphant look on her beautiful face. The court had agreed with Shandra and granted a preliminary injunction pending a hearing. She'd won the first round.

Six days later, Mindy was bounced out of school again, feeling like a human ping-pong ball. When her court hearing was held, the judge removed the preliminary injunction, refusing to grant a permanent one. Disappointed, she realized this meant her transfer would stand. Shandra sounded both irritated and frustrated when Mindy talked to her. "I'm sorry," Shandra said. "I thought I could keep you in the classroom."

"I know you did your best. Does this mean we've lost?" Mindy asked.

"Nope," Shandra replied. "Your court date's been scheduled for mid-June." She paused before saying, "The opposition threatened to fire you as a way of settling the dispute."

Mindy's bottom puckered. Shandra said, "They were bluffing. I told them we're ready to file a lawsuit in the double-digit millions if they fire you, since you're tenured. They pulled in their horns."

"Meaning?"

"Meaning," Shandra explained, "they've conceded your transfer is temporary and you'll be returned to the classroom next fall. You're stuck in the records office until then. I can't do a thing about that."

After Mindy's bottom unpuckered she said, "Shandra, I appreciate all you've done for me. I would've been lost without you."

"It's been a two-way street," Shandra corrected softly. "I've met some people with the A.C.L.U. because of you. If I play my cards right I can turn your case into the job of my dreams, now that I have connections." Then she added, "Don't you worry, we're gonna give 'em hell!"

The next day Cheerio and Mindy moved back home and Mindy went back to her job at the cumulative records office. Back to the dusty file cabinets and the thrill of transferring letters and numbers from one piece of paper to another. She felt bored and worthless and wasted every minute of every day. And she missed her kids.

It was in Mindy's eighth month, in April, when she and Cheerio enrolled in a natural childbirth class. They only got to go to two classes. When they went to the third class and spread their blanket and pillow out on the floor with the other couples, the instructor came in and motioned them outside. "You're disrupting the entire class," the instructor pronounced coldly when they were out in the hall. "Everyone keeps watching you instead of listening to me. They're not learning a thing."

"But," Mindy said, "I explained my situation to everyone. I also explained how my cousin agreed to be my coach."

"I've watched how you touch each other and how you talk to each other," the instructor said. "If you're cousins, I'm a monkey's uncle."

"I notice the family resemblance," Cheerio commented dryly.

"Could we arrange for you to give us a separate class?" Mindy asked. "For just us so we couldn't distract anyone?"

The instructor snapped, "You've got to be kidding," and stomped back into the classroom. Mindy said, "I suppose we'll have to leave our blanket and pillow. I'd be embarrassed to walk back in there after she not-so-politely booted us out."

"No big deal," Cheerio grunted, and boldly marched into the classroom. All the students started nudging each other and whispering. The instructor snapped, "Didn't I make myself clear, Miss Monroe?"

"We're not leaving without our blanket and pillow," Cheerio snapped back in her best haughty tone. She threw the blanket over her shoulder, tucked the pillow under her arm and headed toward the door. She veered away all of a sudden, walked over to the instructor, winked, pinched her bottom and said, "Could you drop by earlier than normal tonight, hon? I'm dying to be with you."

The instructor jumped, dropped her doll and started backing away. "I...we...I...we," she sputtered. Mindy chuckled at the scene from the doorway.

They ended up finding a retired nurse who gave them the lessons and wrote them a nice certificate when they completed the course.

*****

Cheerio dressed all in white, from head to foot. White dress, hose, heels. She put her stage makeup on and fixed her hair. Ten rings went on her fingers and an ankle bracelet went around her left ankle. It was the same outfit she'd worn the last time she performed with Cappie. She'd saved it all these years, nine years, because it made Cappie still seem alive. Sure enough, it was a way of denying that Cappie had died, a way of making her think that fucked-up night in New York when they'd overdosed, had never happened.

She was going to wear the outfit one more time, one final time in honor of Cappie, and then she was going to put the outfit to rest. And she was, finally, going to put Cappie to rest.

Cheerio walked into the great room. Mindy was sleeping sitting up on the couch. She was snoring softly, a trickle of slobber was running down her chin. Spike was sleeping in her lap. Cheerio touched Mindy's cheek, feeling so much love it almost made her feel like she was about to overdose on feelings.

Mindy's eyes flickered opened. Cheerio caught her breath at the...fear...she saw in the brown depths. The fear quickly vanished and was replaced by calmness. Cheerio felt like taking Mindy in her arms and holding her close because Mindy had been through so much the past few months, but hadn't backed off a bit. The dyke had a spine like stainless steel. Fear would never get the better of her.

"Have I been asleep?" Mindy asked, wiping at the slobber on her chin and looking embarrassed.

"Yes, baby," Cheerio said softly.

Mindy stared at the way Cheerio was dressed, her eyes flickering again in confusion. "I'm going down to The Eager Beaver," Cheerio said, feeling cold-blooded calm.

"Why? I'm sorry I fell asleep. I feel rested now. We can do something. Go to a late movie or something."

"I talked to Alysa a while ago," Cheerio said. "The joint is packed. I'm about half-ass nervous." She pointed to the coffee table. "I set out a glass of orange juice and some cookies for you for a bedtime snack."

"What are you saying?"

"No bunch of drunks are going to jeer me off a stage and get away with it," Cheerio replied, feeling bitter because she had been a *star* at one time and she could be a *star* again if she wanted to. The talent was still there, and she was god-damn sure enough going to prove it to everybody. And to herself. "Eat your snack and go to bed. I'll be back in a couple of hours to tell you all about it." She kissed her fingers, pressed them to Mindy's lips and left.

*****

Mindy sat quietly on the couch for maybe fifteen minutes after Cheerio left, feeling stunned. "Bull-shit," she finally said. "I'm not missing this, even if I am as big as the Hindenburg." She rolled around on the couch for about five minutes before she finally managed to stand up. Grabbing her purse, she waddled out to her car and sped to The Eager Beaver.

The Eager Beaver *was* packed. Mindy had to park two blocks away. It took her somewhere in the neighborhood of six weeks to waddle the two blocks because she had to stop and rest twice. Her ankles and feet were killing her by the time she finally got there. The smoke inside was so dense she decided to dock right beside the door so she could push it open a crack and get a breath of fresh air every so often.

The whole place was dark, except for the stage and behind the bar, where Sherry and Jo worked under a dim yellowish light, fixing drinks and slapping them down as fast as they could work. The stage was lit in white and blue and red lights beyond the thick haze of smoke. Fawn was standing stock-still in the center of the stage, holding a microphone with one hand. Her other hand hung at her side. She was singing a melancholy love song in a high, soaring voice. It sounded strange, out of place, because Silky Wet's music was the kind of Southern watermelon-boogie that made everyone go wild, and wasn't really suited to melancholy love songs or a high, soaring voice.

When Fawn finished her song, there was a smattering of applause that could barely be heard over everyone talking. Even the people who were clapping were talking and not really paying attention, although a few people did stop talking long enough to scream rude propositions at Fawn. Fawn ran to Alysa, wringing her hands, tears in her beautiful eyes. Alysa patted her shoulder.

Cheerio appeared from behind the drums, looking like an angel with her white clothes, the different-colored lights shining on her hair. She snatched the microphone out of its stand and roared, "You gash-tails shut the fuck up so we can rock-and-roll!"

Everyone stopped talking and started staring.

"That's more like it!" Cheerio shouted, booting the microphone stand off the stage and into the crowd. Everyone dodged. Cheerio said, "This one's called 'In The Night.' I wrote it for someone I loved who died yesterday. I want to sing it for her today."

Alysa bellowed, "Ladies, let's give-it-fucking-up!"

The keyboard cut loose with a drawn-out 'Zzzzz!' sound and played by itself for a few seconds. Then the drums thumped and the bass guitar and the rhythm guitar joined in and they all played together for a few more seconds. When Alysa's lead guitar kicked in, everyone started dancing. Alysa wasn't a liar when she said she was the best female guitar player in the free world. Her knees were bent, her head was bent over her guitar and she was giving it the dickens. It was a definite sight to see, all the women in the band with their leather pants and all their black and blond, and one orange-tinted, heads of teased hair, bobbing over their instruments, and the ton of moist, breast-wriggling groupies mobbing the front of the stage.

Cheerio cut loose about this time, in a voice so powerful it practically blew the roof off The Eager Beaver. The music changed gears and got more frenzied, with Alysa's guitar snapping around the edges of Cheerio's voice. Cheerio's voice was snarling and a little taunting. She pranced back-and-forth with an arrogant look on her face, running a hand over her body, touching her breasts, her crotch, her bottom, flaunting herself in front of all the women. Her song was about waking up and reaching for someone in the night, but they weren't there and they'd never be there again and it broke your heart and you felt like hurting someone, anyone, even yourself, because you were hurting so badly.

But Cheerio's song wasn't a melancholy love song. It was an angry, emotional song instead. When it ended, the place exploded. Everyone was screaming and whistling and clapping. Everyone except Fawn. She looked stunned, and tears streamed down her cheeks. She turned away and fought her way through the crowd toward the bathroom.

Cheerio shouted, "Fuck you very much!" Everyone jeered. A beer can landed on the stage. Cheerio booted it back into the crowd. It bounced off the head of a tall blond with big breasts wearing a purple sequined gown, who must've really been a man because he/she roared, "God-damn-son-of-a-bitch!" in a baritone. The women around him/her jerked a wig off his/her head, poured beer on him/her and shoved him/her toward the door.

Cheerio shouted, "You lying bitches know you want it! Dream on, babes!" She licked a finger, pressed it against her bottom and said, "Sssss. This sweet stuff is too hot for any of you to handle. It'd burn the enamel off your teeth." Everyone cracked up. Cheerio smirked because she knew she had everyone eating out of her hand.

About this time, Mindy got swept out the door with the him/her in the purple sequined gown, along with several other people. She decided to just keep waddling toward her car since she was already heading in that direction. She'd seen what she came to see, anyway.

Halfway home, the first contraction came. Mindy was stopped for a red light. She gasped and bent her head to the steering wheel. It was so strange, so surrealistic. The bright lights around the intersection were blurred by her tears. She couldn't breathe; the people behind her leaned on their horns because the light turned green and she didn't pull away. Cars with fist-shaking drivers drove past. And all the time her stomach was ripping her in two.

The pain lessened in a minute and she managed to get her car going, practically moving as fast as grass grows. Her face felt wet, whether from tears or sweat she didn't know. Two blocks from home the second contraction came. The whole surrealistic scene staged a repeat performance. She started to turn around and drive to the hospital but didn't. "I'm not going there by myself," she said to nobody but herself.

She managed to make it the rest of the way home and staggered into the house, bent double and maybe bellowing a curse word or two about Cheerio being gone, about God's cruelty, about the whole damn situation. Spike started running around and yapping as soon as she walked in the door. Mindy sat on the couch and held the furry little body until she got a grip on herself.

When she could breathe again, she waddled to the kitchen for a glass of orange juice and a wet paper towel to wipe her face. After that, she waddled to the bathroom and deposited the orange juice in the toilet via her stomach and mouth. The second she finished depositing her orange juice in the toilet she made an unladylike blurping sound with her bottom. "How rude!" she exclaimed. "I'm glad nobody was here to hear. Then added, "I'm lying. I wish somebody was here to hear."

Spike yapped, hung out her tongue and cocked her head. "You don't count," Mindy said. She snatched up the phone, called The Eager Beaver and got a busy signal. She pulled out her address book and started making calls to take her mind off her practically dire straits. Her contractions were exactly eight minutes apart. She called Dr. Marks and got mumbled profanity followed by a yawning, "You're early. I'll be right there," followed by a woman's voice yelling, "Not again! Why didn't I marry an accountant!" Cheerio's family was next. She got sleepy concern and excitement about a new grandchild. Shandra was next, only to talk to an answering machine. The Eager Beaver's line was still busy.

Shortly after hanging up the phone, Cheerio and Alysa and Fawn and the women from Silky Wet came boiling in the door. It was three in the morning. Everyone was meowing their fool heads off. Mindy was sitting on the floor with her back propped against the couch and her knees lifted, wishing she could get her panties off so she could go ahead and get the thing over with. Her mouth dropped open in amazement when she saw how everyone ignored her so they could meow at each other. Spike must have been amazed, too, because she sped in a circle around and around the group, yapping like anything.

Fawn sat on the couch, looking as amazed as Mindy felt and Spike was acting. She pulled a nail file from her purse, curled her legs under her and went to alternating between filing her nails, watching the fight, and watching Mindy watching the fight and trying to remember her breathing exercises at the same time. Fawn finally said, "My mother acted like you're acting when she had my sister. Tell me when you're ready and we'll go to the hospital." She blinked once, slowly, and went back to filing her nails.

Mindy didn't say anything because Cheerio shouted, "Get off my ass, Alysa! I'm not flying to New York with you tonight!" loud enough to wake the dead.

Alysa's makeup was streaked like she'd been crying, although she was tough as nails and Mindy couldn't imagine her crying over anything. "Didn't you hear those people cheering for you?" Alysa roared. "Doesn't that sound get inside of you? You're wasting a gift. A gift very few people have. You've hoarded away twelve of the best songs I've ever heard. That's more than enough to make an album."

"Are you deaf or what?" Cheerio shouted.

Alysa clutched Cheerio's arm and said, "Just the two of us. We'll make a fortune in no time and come back here to retire."

"What about Mindy?"

"She's going," Alysa said, waving a hand in the general direction of Mindy without bothering to look. "That goes without saying."

Thumper, the raw-boned drummer with orange-tinted hair, huge orange glasses and buckteeth, snatched a handful of Alysa's hair and screeched, "I'm going, too, Mary Jane Smith! We've played together since we were kids! You're not ditching me now!"

The other band members screeched, "We're all going or you're a dead dyke!"

"Fine!" Alysa shouted, waving her arms. "We'll all go. Fawn, too. She can do the backup vocals on the album. Now shut up your sniveling." She snatched the front of Thumper's blouse, pulled her close and hissed, "Don't ever call me Mary Jane Smith again. I hate that fucking name!"

"I'll do my own backups!" Cheerio shouted. She pulled at her hair with both hands. "What am I saying? I'm not going anywhere."

Mindy arched her back, tried to puff but instead screamed, "Ooohhh, lawsy! Here we go again!" She slapped the egg timer she was using to time her contractions.

All of a sudden everyone stopped fighting. They all gathered in a semicircle around Mindy and stared down at her with open mouths and wide eyes. Cheerio, since she was practically a rocket scientist, asked, "What do you think you're doing down there?"

"Just what does it look like I'm doing down here?" Mindy panted. "I think I'm having my baby!" She wanted to cry but started laughing instead. Life was just too funny to take seriously. It really was. Actually, though, it was too serious to laugh about.

Alysa, since she was no slouch herself when it came to rockets, gnawed a fingernail and tentatively asked, "You're really going through with this thing?"

"I feel so basic," Mindy panted. "I'm going to reproduce just like an animal. And I can't even go off by myself under a bush somewhere. I'm going to reproduce in front of practically the whole world!"

"But you're not due for another week," Cheerio said dumbly. She squatted and peered into Mindy's face. Her eyes looked amused. "Why are you laughing and crying? Are you having a nervous breakdown?"

"Are you crazy?" Mindy panted. "I've never felt so much pain in my life. But, still, I've never felt so alive. I feel so in touch with my senses. All five of them. It's the greatest sensation!"

Everyone stared down at her like she had three 36D's.

Everyone except Alysa. Alysa snatched up the phone, waved her free hand in the air and screeched, "Operator! Fire Department! Ambulance! We're having a baby! This is serious shit!" without even dialing a number.

Cheerio rolled her eyes. "Give me that thing, Mary," she said. "We'll handle this ourselves." She snatched the phone and hung it up.

Alysa tossed her head and snapped, "Well, just go fuck yourself, Cheerio Monroe. I'm only trying to help. What do you think we should do?"

"Well," Cheerio said, looking thoughtful.

Everyone looked at Mindy.

"Goofy women," Mindy mumbled, shaking her head. "Let's get to the hospital."

They had to form a three-car caravan to the hospital to have room for everyone. Mindy kept her eyes closed practically all the way because Cheerio blew through maybe a zillion stop lights and stop signs on the way. The nurses at the hospital practically dropped their teeth when they saw a herd of leather-pant-wearing, teased-hair, makeup-streaked women galloping into the emergency room at a quarter-to-four in the morning, screaming their heads off, except for Mindy who was crying and laughing with one arm wrapped around Thumper's shoulders and the other around Alysa's, since they were the tallest. All this as Cheerio was speeding ahead to get the paperwork started.

Alysa all of a sudden blurted, "I can't believe I trashed my Les Paul tonight! It was my favorite axe!"

"Then why'd you smash it all over the stage for?" Thumper asked.

"You tell me." Alysa looked embarrassed for probably the first time in her life. "I just plain got caught up in the spirit of things when Cheerio put her foot through your bass drum."

"It definitely got different there at the end," Thumper agreed. She rubbed Mindy's bottom and whispered, "How you making it, sugar tit? Motherhood must agree with you. You're looking good enough to eat raw this morning."

"Yeah, right," Mindy said. She laughed because she saw Sherry and Jo coming down the hall, holding hands and chugging along as fast as their stubby legs could go. The mother-to-be gave a happy sigh, for now all her friends were around her.

The next person she saw was her doctor. Dr. Marks was yawning and scratching her head and sipping a cup of coffee. "Your timing's for the birds," she grumbled. "Is there a law against having babies during normal office hours? Is there? Can anyone answer that question? I can't. Why didn't I go into electrical engineering? I'm charging quadruple overtime for this."

A nurse led Cheerio away to change into her coaching clothes. Two other nurses put Mindy in a wheelchair and steered her into Birthing Room Number Three.

CHAPTER 11

It was about an hour until sunset. The sun was just at the top of the privacy fence. The sky was the kind of pale, bluish-grey it always was right before sunset. There wasn't a cloud in sight.

Barefoot Cheerio was sitting in a lawn chair, sipping an iced tea and teasing Spike, who was jumping around in a corner of the backyard, yapping her little head off. A robin was perched on top of the fence above Spike, cleaning itself, and pretty much ignoring Spike because Spike was practically as threatening as an earthworm.

Mindy was stretched out on the glider, swinging slowly back-and-forth and feeling so peaceful it was practically disgusting and probably illegal. She was stylishly attired in a pink bathrobe. Since nobody was watching to laugh at her anxiety, she counted Shannon's tiny toes and fingers for the zillionth time. She was a mathematician, after all. Correct numbers mattered to her a great deal.

After the digit count, Mindy traced a finger across Shannon's round little face and arms. Shannon's skin was so soft that Mindy felt obliged to whisper, "I don't suppose you'd like to trade skin with Mama, would you?" She stroked Shannon's head. The wispy brown hair was fine, like silky thread. Shannon's eyes were greyish-colored now, but Mindy knew they would probably change before she was much older.

Mindy felt a shadow fall across her face and all of a sudden realized she wasn't as unobserved as she'd thought. Looking up, she saw Cheerio standing there. "Time's up," Cheerio said greedily. "My turn to hold our daughter."

"Well, okay," Mindy sighed. She ran a finger across Shannon's cheek and kissed a silky forehead before surrendering her. Mindy felt anxious, for no reason, of course, as Cheerio took Shannon and returned to her lawn chair. Cheerio cooed softly and jiggled her arms. A sweet smile appeared on her face when she folded back the blanket to look at Shannon's face.

Then Alysa and Fawn made their grand entrance; they were all dolled-up for work. Completely ignoring Mindy, they made a beeline for Cheerio and the darling of the household. They squatted beside Cheerio, one on each side, and gushed baby-talk at Shannon.

Miss Brandi Brinson pranced out on the patio right behind Alysa and Fawn, in a swirling display of long brown hair and swelling breasts inside a white cropped top and a taut midriff. The lean, tan legs seemed to go on forever. "Hi, sis," Mindy said. "Don't you look nice tonight?" Brandi smiled a heartbreaking smile. "How tall are you now?" Mindy asked.

"Five-eleven," Brandi sighed. "I hope I've stopped growing."

"Pooh-pooh," Mindy said. "You're a runt."

"I'm going," Brandi announced. "Jimmy's here to take me to the show. We're going to play miniature golf afterwards, and we'll probably go to Pizza Hut so I can meet his friends."

"When do *I* get to meet this boy you're so crazy about?"

"Mindy!" Brandi put her hands on her hips and stamped a foot. "If you make me drag him out here to meet you like you're my mother, I'll just absolutely die of embarrassment."

Mindy laughed. The cute way Brandi cocked her head and said, '*I'll just absolutely die!*' was touching. It reminded her of when they'd been children and Brandi would say she'd '*just absolutely die!*' if she didn't get to do something.

"Please," Brandi said, touching Mindy's cheek.

"Okay, okay," Mindy said. "I'm just being careful. When Mother and Daddy agreed to let you spend the summer with me, I had to promise not to let you get corrupted. I'm just keeping my promise to them. Besides, I'm not so sure I think very much of a boy who picked you up in the produce section at Skaggs. I'm also not sure I think much of you for letting yourself get picked up in the produce section at Skaggs, you little trollop."

"I'm eighteen years old," Brandi said, stamping a foot again. "An adult. You'll just have to trust me."

"I know when I'm beat," Mindy grumbled. "But you *will* be home no later than twelve o'clock. If you're not, I'm grounding you for the next ten centuries."

"Okay-fine," Brandi said.

"Behave yourself. No back seats and dark streets."

Brandi rolled her eyes. A sly look crossed her face. "I almost forgot to ask you a favor," she said coyly. "I'm out of condoms. Do you have some you could loan me?"

Everyone hooted.

Except Mindy. She felt practically disgusted. She tried to slap Brandi's arm, but Brandi pranced away too quickly. She moved to Cheerio, smiled her heartbreaking smile at everyone, and bent to kiss Shannon before prancing back into the house to her boyfriend, amid a chorus of wistful feminine sighs.

"Your sister has one of the ten best tushes in the free world," Alysa said.

"I know," Mindy agreed. "Don't you just hate her?"

"Not hardly," Alysa said, heaving another sigh. Cheerio and Fawn heaved sighs, too.

"What are you sighing for, Cheerio?" Alysa asked scoldingly. "You sleep with a world-class tush every night."

"So do you," Cheerio said. "Mary Jane Smith."

"Well, just go bleep yourself, Cheerio Monroe," Alysa said, tossing her head, remembering the new rule about no cussing around the baby.

Fawn straightened, swept her hair behind a shoulder, walked to the glider and sat beside Mindy. "Hi, there, sweet pea," Mindy said. "Don't you look nice tonight? I love your gold blouse. It's darling."

"Thank you." Fawn picked up Mindy's legs and laid them across her lap. She slipped her hands inside Mindy's robe and started tickling her feet and calves. Mindy practically purred. She loved having her legs tickled. Everyone had been spoiling the dickens out of her during the four weeks she'd been home from the hospital.

"Please don't forget to use your breast-pump in the morning," Fawn said, a pleading look in her eyes. "I'm so anxious to hold Shannon and feed her. You promised you'd let me."

"I haven't forgotten."

"Thank you for breakfast," Fawn said shyly. "It was delicious, as usual. I love your blueberry pancakes and the cinnamon-flavored oatmeal you cook. Alysa and I did the dishes after we finished."

"Thanks," Mindy said, knowing full well who'd done the dishes. Alysa thought dishes went in the trash like a golden arches box when you were through with them. "Let's see," Mindy said. "Last night you were just starting to tell me about your family when you had to go to work."

"I remember," Fawn said. "My father is Japanese-American, my mother Polynesian. I have one younger sister and one younger brother." She paused and smiled at Cheerio, Shannon and Alysa. Her fingernails traced circles on Mindy's legs. "I miss everyone in my family except my father," Fawn continued after a few seconds. "He told me if I left with Alysa I should never come back because I've disgraced the family." Her eyes looked moist. "I tried to explain that I had to come to the mainland and meet people, how I could never get my big break on the islands. He wouldn't listen. He took off his belt and tried to beat me. I took my suitcase and left."

"How horrible." Mindy brushed at several strands of loose hair on Fawn's cheek.

"I'd rather not talk about that," Fawn said, her voice softer than usual. Her fingernails moved slowly up Mindy's legs. "I'd rather talk about how much I love living here. Your home is so pleasant. I love the way it's centered around the kitchen. Your kitchen always smells like boiling beans or frying bacon or brewing coffee. And the way you keep fried chicken wrapped in foil in the refrigerator. Sometimes I sneak into the kitchen when nobody's watching and take the chicken out of the refrigerator just to smell it, just to convince myself I'm not dreaming because the chicken is really there and I'm really alive and living in a place so wonderful. I feel loved every time I walk into your kitchen and see you standing at the stove or in front of the sink, trading pretend insults with anyone who walks in."

"Oh, stop it," Mindy said. "I'm practically blushing."

"I'm talking simple things," Fawn said. Her fingernails tickled higher on Mindy's legs. "Simple smells. Everyday things. Just everyday life going on. Can you imagine what these things and smells mean to someone from a home with an abusive father? What chicken in foil means to me? When I'm in your kitchen with you I can forget my childhood. When I'm around you I think it's the best place in the world to be and I hate to think about ever leaving. I feel like the luckiest wahine in the world."

"I wonder if I feel like blubbering," Mindy said. "You've made me feel so good." Fawn flashed one of her brilliant smiles. She shifted closer, face lowered, eyes glinting under her lashes. Her fingernails reached Mindy's thighs. The inside of Mindy's thighs. Mindy's crotch, actually.

Mindy took the delicate brown hands, kissed them and gave them a squeeze. "Are you making a pass at an old witch like me?" she asked. "Right here in front of the love of my life?"

Fawn blinked once, slowly. "You're too intelligent to be as naive about your looks as you act," she said. "I love Alysa, but I wouldn't say no if you came on to me. I couldn't say no."

Cheerio's head snapped around. "Some little chicken's close to getting her neck wrung," she meowed.

Fawn presented her part to Cheerio. "I'm sorry," she said. "But it's the way I feel. I'm being honest."

"Wrap it in foil," Cheerio snapped.

Alysa stood, walked to the glider, grabbed Mindy's cheeks and planted a kiss right smack dab on her mouth. Mindy felt Alysa's tongue against her lips so she pulled back and said, "You cheap hussy."

Alysa laughed. Her eyes flashed. She walked back to Cheerio and planted a kiss smack dab on Cheerio's mouth. Mindy watched to see if Cheerio opened her mouth during the kiss so she could turn green if she had to. Cheerio didn't open her mouth and Mindy was relieved she didn't have to turn green. She wasn't in a green mood.

Shannon got a kiss next. Then Alysa walked back to the glider and planted a kiss smack dab on Fawn's mouth. Fawn's mouth instantly popped open and she wrapped her arms around Alysa's waist.

"What's this all about?" Mindy asked. "What did we do to deserve kisses?" Alysa put on an absolutely foolish smile. "Ain't love great?" she practically chortled.

"Cheerio, will you come and sing with us tonight?" Fawn asked, focusing hero-worshipping eyes on Cheerio. "I wish you would. I learn so much every time I watch you perform."

"We'll see," Cheerio said noncommittally.

Alysa took Fawn's hand and they left about the time Spike gave up on trying to terrify the robin. The furball trotted to the patio, flopped down and lolled her miniature tongue out. She looked exhausted from her bird-terrifying.

"I want you to quit smoking," Mindy said. "At least at home. That's not a good example for our daughter."

"That's the straw that broke my back," Cheerio said. "I'm outta here." She didn't make a move to leave, though. They sat quietly for a while, just like an old complacent married couple. Mindy finally said, "I thought you were outta here."

"I'm where I want to be or I wouldn't be here," Cheerio said.

"Don't go out tonight," Mindy begged. "We'll feed Shannon in a bit and bathe her and put her to sleep. Then I'll fix us some popcorn and we can curl up on the couch and watch a movie. Seems like we haven't been alone in forever."

"It's not my fault," Cheerio said, pretending to be disgusted. "You're the one who surrounded us with a menagerie of people."

"Au contraire, my little chicken," Mindy said breezily. "You've had as big a part in building our nest as I have."

"Nervous about going to court next week?"

"Not really," Mindy said. "Shandra said all I have to do is get up on the stand and answer her questions and tell my side of the story. It doesn't sound all that scary. I suppose I don't feel any pressure because I don't care about the money. I'll gladly settle for an apology and a change in the pregnancy policy."

Shannon woke up and whimpered. Actually, she woke up and proceeded to squall at the top of her lungs, but Mindy wasn't about to admit any daughter of hers would squall at the top of her lungs. Cheerio put Shannon on the picnic table to change her diaper. But Shannon only squalled louder and flailed the air with her tiny fists. Spike cocked her head and watched with a great deal of interest. Mindy felt like she was about to explode from neurotic anxiety. She wasn't a total fool, though, so she didn't interfere. Interfering with a mother and her infant was a good way to lose a finger real quick.

Cheerio moved to the glider. "Shut this thing up, would you," she said in mock gruffness, handing Shannon over to Mindy.

Mindy quickly undid her robe and popped a breast into Shannon's mouth. Popping a breast into that tiny mouth had been hard the first few times, but Mama was a real pro now. Mama could practically feel Shannon's suckling clear down to her toenails. It felt like her soul was flowing into Shannon's body along with the milk.

Cheerio sat on the glider and held Shannon's hand while she ate. "We'll have a lot of explaining to do to her someday," Cheerio murmured.

"We'll worry about that time when it comes," Mindy said, squeezing Cheerio's arm.

"Can Fawn tickle as good as me?"

"Of course not." Mindy shifted and threw her legs across Cheerio's lap. "Do your thing, blondie," she ordered. Tickle-tickle-tickle went Cheerio's fingernails. Mindy practically purred. She also felt a lustful warmth in her crotch that hadn't been there during Fawn's tickling so she felt obliged to say, "Will you violate me later? Coarsely and with complete disregard for my human dignity? Pretty please?"

"I love you," Cheerio murmured. "I can't say it as nice as Fawn, but you know how I feel."

"I love you, too, you insecure little thing."

Cheerio leaned back with a smile. A few seconds later she started singing a trembly-chinned knuckle-sucking love song she'd written the night after Shannon's birth. Her voice gradually grew stronger and drifted over the fence, across the neighbor's houses and toward the stars.

Mindy looked around, at all the precious pieces of her life. Her lover. Their daughter. Their home. Their dog. She smiled to herself. She thought the backyard was filled just right.

For the time being, anyway.

The End

Other Books From Rising Tide Press

RETURN TO ISIS
Jean Stewart

The year is 2093. In this fantasy zone where sword and superstition meet sci-fi adventure, two women make a daring escape to freedom. Whit, a bold warrior from an Amazon nation, rescues Amelia from a dismal world where females are either breeders or drones.

Together, they journey over grueling terrain, to the shining world of Artemis, and in their struggle to survive, find themselves unexpectedly drawn to each other.

But it is in the safety of Artemis, Whit's home colony, that danger truly lurks. For beneath Amelia's haunting dreams hides a secret which cannot be allowed to surface. A secret of Isis, the colony mysteriously destroyed ten years earlier. And in the ruins of Isis is the ghost of a fallen Leader who has been waiting for Amelia's return.

If you liked *Daughters of a Coral Dawn*, you'll love this entertaining tale of high adventure, mystery and love, by a bright new face on the sci-fi scene. Look for the sequel.

$8.95   **ISBN 0-962893-6-2**

****

FACES OF LOVE
Sharon Gilligan

A wise and sensitive novel which takes us into the lives of Maggie, Karen, Cory, and their community of friends. Maggie Halloran, a prominent women's rights advocate, and Karen Weston, a brilliant attorney, have been together for 10 years in a relationship full of love and conflict. When Maggie's heart is captured by the young and beautiful Cory, she must take stock of her life and make some difficult decisions.

Set against the backdrop of Madison, Wisconsin, the characters in this engaging novel are bright, involved, '90's women dealing with universal issues of love, commitment and friendship.

$8.95   **ISBN 09628938-4-6**

More Books from Rising Tide Press

ROMANCING THE DREAM
Heidi Johanna

Author and journalist, H.H. Johanna, makes her debut as a novelist with **Romancing the Dream**—a captivating and erotic love story—with an unusual twist.

This imaginative tale begins when Jacqui St. John leaves northern California looking for a new home, and cruises into the seemingly ordinary town of Kulshan. Seeing the lilac bushes blooming along the roadside, she suddenly remembers the recurring dream that has been tantalizing her for months—a dream of a house full of women, radiating warmth and welcome, and of one special woman dressed in silk and leather.

But why has Jacqui, like so many other women been drawn to this town? The answer is simple, but startling—the women plan to take control of this little Oregon town and make it a haven for Lesbians.

$8.95   **ISBN 0-9628938-0-3**

****

EDGE OF PASSION
Shelley Smith

From the moment Angela saw Mickey sitting at the end of the smoky bar at the Blue Moon Cafe, she was consumed with desire for this cool and sophisticated woman, and determined to have her...at any cost.

Set against the backdrop of colorful Provincetown, this sizzling novel will draw you into the all-consuming love affair between an older and younger woman, and will keep you breathless until the last page.

$8.95   **ISBN 0-9628938-1-1**

ORDERING INFORMATION

These books are available at your local feminist or Lesbian/gay bookstore, or directly from **Rising Tide Press**. Orders under $25, send check or money order. Orders **over** $25 may also be charged to Visa/MC using our **Toll-Free** number: **1-800-648-5333**. If mailing charge orders in, please include account number, expiration date, signature. Charge orders shipped in 48 hours. All mail-in orders please include **$4.50** for shipping & handling. Send check or money order in U.S. funds to **Rising Tide Press, 5 Kivy St., Huntington Station, NY 11746**

If You Liked This Book...

Authors seldom get to hear what readers like about their work. If you enjoyed this novel, **You Light The Fire**, why not let the author know? We are sure she would be delighted to get your feedback. Simply write the author:

Kristen Garrett
c/o Rising Tide Press
5 Kivy Street
Huntington Station, NY 11746

RISING TIDE PRESS

OUR PUBLISHING PHILOSOPHY

Rising Tide Press is a Lesbian-owned and operated publishing company committed to publishing books for, by and about Lesbians, and their lives. We are not only committed to readers, but also to Lesbian writers who need nurturing and support, whether or not their manuscripts are accepted for publication. Through quality writing, the press aims to entertain, educate, and empower readers, whether they are women-loving-women or heterosexual. It is our intention to promote Lesbian culture, community, and civil rights, nationwide, through the printed word.

In addition, RTP will seek to provide readers with images of Lesbians aspiring to be more than their prescribed roles dictate. The novels selected for publication will aim to portray women from all walks of life, (regardless of class, ethnicity, religion or race), women who are strong, not just victims, women who can and do aspire to become more, and not just settle, women who will fight injustice with courage. Hopefully, our novels will provide new ideas for creating change, in a heterosexist and homophobic society. Finally, we hope our books will encourage Lesbians to respect and love themselves more, and at the same time, convey this love and respect of self to the society at large. It is our belief that this philosophy can best be actualized through fine writing that entertains, as well as educates the reader. Books, even Lesbian books, can be fun, as well as liberating.

If you share our vision of a better Lesbian future, and would like to become a part of a network helping to promote these publishing goals, please consider making a contribution, any amount appreciated, to Rising Tide Press, so that we may continue this important work into the future.